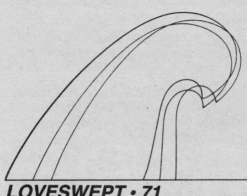

LOVESWEPT · 71

Kay Hooper
If There Be Dragons

BANTAM BOOKS
TORONTO · NEW YORK · LONDON · SYDNEY · AUCKLAND

IF THERE BE DRAGONS
A Bantam Book / December 1984

*LOVESWEPT and the wave device are trademarks of
Bantam Books, Inc.*

ISBN 0-553-21678-3

Published simultaneously in the United States and Canada

PRINTED IN THE UNITED STATES OF AMERICA

O   0 9 8 7 6 5 4 3 2 1

"You're stuck with me, Brooke."

His voice was soft, his gaze level and calm. "I've waited too long just to walk away because of a few lousy dragons."

"Waited?" She had the uneasy feeling that his silence on a certain unnerving subject was about to be broken. And she was right.

"For love," he said simply.

"You don't love me, Cody." Brooke put every ounce of certainty she could muster into the words. "Because you don't know me. Maybe you think you're in love, but you aren't. Love at first sight's a myth. It—"

"It wasn't at first sight," Cody said quietly. "It took a few minutes."

She ignored that. "You can't love someone without knowing them, and you don't know me! We only met last night!"

"Brooke, stop telling me that I can't feel what I feel."

"Well, I'm sorry, but I don't feel what you feel, and I won't ever feel that way. I'm just not interested, period."

The next thing she knew, Brooke found herself hauled against his chest, and locked in an embrace that was inescapable.

"This is the second time I've held you," he said huskily, "but this time I don't feel at all protective . . . or soothing."

"Cody!" She pushed against his chest, disconcerted by the way her senses flared at the contact with unyielding muscles. But then her senses overloaded in a burst of inner sparks as his mouth found hers. . . .

WHAT ARE *LOVESWEPT* ROMANCES?

They are stories of true romance and touching emotion. We believe those two very important ingredients are constants in our highly sensual and very believable stories in the *LOVESWEPT* line. Our goal is to give you, the reader, stories of consistently high quality that may sometimes make you laugh, sometimes make you cry, but are always fresh and creative and contain many delightful surprises within their pages.

Most romance fans read an enormous number of books. Those they truly love, they keep. Others may be traded with friends and soon forgotten. We hope that each *LOVESWEPT* romance will be a treasure—a "keeper." We will always try to publish

LOVE STORIES YOU'LL NEVER FORGET
BY AUTHORS YOU'LL ALWAYS REMEMBER

The Editors

To Bob
for a voice out of the darkness

Prologue

"Please, Cody? You're the only troubleshooter I know!"

"I'm a *business* troubleshooter, Pepper," Cody replied in exasperation to the voice on the other end of the phone.

"You're a *trouble*shooter," his best friend's wife insisted stubbornly. "And Brooke's got trouble. I know you can help her, Cody. If nothing else, you still owe me for foisting that blasted cat onto us!"

Cody laughed. "How is King Tut?"

"Impossible!" Pepper said roundly. "He brought his girlfriend home last night; I've never heard such a racket! And stop changing the subject. Look, you can— Hang on a minute, okay?"

Listening intently Cody heard her say to someone else, "I'm fine, Thor. Stop fussing!" He waited until she came back on the line, then asked in amusement, "What's he worried about? Or should I ask, How's my unborn godchild?"

Pepper laughed suddenly. "Better start thinking in the plural. The doctor hit us with that possibility today, and Thor's coming unraveled."

"I am not!" an indignant male voice announced offstage.

"Twins?" Cody asked in astonishment.

"It looks like it," Pepper confirmed, sounding delighted by the idea.

"I am *not* coming unraveled!" the offstage voice denied firmly.

Half into the receiver and half to Thor, Pepper said, laughing, "Then stop putting pillows behind me and staring at me as if I'm about to explode, darling! We've got two more months to go."

"The doctor said the birth might be early!"

"Not two months early."

Listening to the ensuing "discussion" between his friends, Cody was both amused and envious. Like himself, Thor had spent a large part of his adult life alone. Then Pepper had breezed into the picture, bringing with her an attack-trained Chihuahua, a neurotic Doberman, a huge motor home, and more nutty friends than one young woman should have been able to acquire in her short lifetime.

Thor went down for the count.

Cody thought of Pepper's unabashed and cheerful pursuit of his friend, and that thought prompted a sudden suspicion. "Pepper? Pepper!"

She broke off whatever she'd been saying to Thor, coming back on the line with an amused "Sorry, Cody!"

"That's okay." He voiced his suspicion. "Look, you aren't trying to fix me up with this Brooke, are you?"

Pepper laughed. "I'd love to, Cody, but you're not at all her type. In fact, she's liable to be hostile toward you."

Taken aback, Cody demanded, "Then why should I try to help her?"

"As a favor to me. Please, Cody?"

Irritably reflecting that it was difficult to say no when Pepper pleaded so sweetly, Cody nonetheless tried. "I've got a month's vacation coming up, and—"

"That's perfect!" Pepper interrupted cheerfully. "You can go up to Brooke's and—"

"—and I'd planned to take a cruise!" Cody finished defiantly.

Pepper was silent for a moment, then she spoke slowly and carefully. "Cody, I don't want to make the situation sound more serious than it may be, but I think Brooke's in real trouble. I can't go up there because the doctor won't let me travel, and Thor can't go. She's all alone, Cody, and I'm worried about her."

Weakening, and unwillingly curious, he asked, "Just exactly what's going on?"

"I don't know." Pepper sounded unusually fretful. "But she's been nervous and edgy lately, and I think she's afraid. There was some kind of trouble right after she inherited the place from an uncle, but I think that was legal stuff. Now . . . I don't know. But something's wrong, and I—"

"Okay, okay," Cody soothed hastily, alarmed and unsettled by the sudden break in her voice. "If it'll make you feel better, little mama, I'll go up there. Just tell me exactly *where* it is I'm supposed to go, and call your friend to announce me. How does that sound?"

* * *

"That was a terrific performance, beloved."

"It wasn't bad, was it?"

"Especially the little heartrending break in your voice."

"I *am* worried, darling."

"I know you are. I also know you've a devious mind and ruthless matchmaking instincts. You were determined to get him and Brooke together, weren't you?"

"Of course."

"You said you'd warn him if you started matchmaking."

"I did—as far as I was able to. He asked if I was trying to fix him up with Brooke, and I said that I'd love to, but that he wasn't her type."

"Liar."

"Not at all, darling. *She* won't think he is her type."

"Lord, you're devious."

"Mmm."

"Why'd you make that face? D'you have a pain?" he asked anxiously.

"No, darling."

"Are you sure?"

Pepper sighed. "Two months is going to pass . . . slowly."

One

There was no answer at the front door. Cody shoved his hands deep into the pockets of his thickly quilted jacket and stepped back from the door, casting a hostile glance out over what would probably be a breathtaking view during daylight. At the moment he could only dimly discern the hulking and intimidating mountains looming all around the tiny valley.

Montana, he was thinking in disgust, and in the middle of winter too! He swore softly, moving out to the edge of the rustic redwood deck that pretended to be a front porch. The durable Jeep that had brought him with relative safety up the winding and icy road to this valley was making soft popping and crackling noises as its hot engine cooled down rapidly in the frigid air. Only those sounds and an occasional whine from the wind high above disturbed the silence.

Cody took care in stepping off the deck, avoiding the two shallow steps, which, he'd discovered only moments before, were slippery. He stood for a moment in the trampled snow that formed a rough walkway, staring at the rented Jeep and then looking around quickly for any sign of a garage. Another building off to one side attracted his attention, and he made his way in that direction cautiously, silently cursing his lack of forethought in not having worn thick boots; his ankle boots just didn't allow for nearly a foot of snow.

He glanced back at the lodge once, trying for the third time to gain some impression of size or style, but was defeated again. The tall trees surrounding the building shadowed it too heavily to offer even a dim silhouette. It was big, though; that much he was sure of. And not a light showed anywhere.

He located a window in the side of the fairly large outbuilding and brushed snow away from the shallow sill, cupping his hands around his eyes and leaning closer for a look inside. The interior was dim, but he felt his brows raise slightly as he identified the hulking shape of a Sno-Cat on the far side. Nearer, he could barely make out a Jeep very like his own but with a more battered appearance.

Cody let his arms drop and backed away from the window, stumbling over rocks bordering a narrow trodden path. Regaining his balance and absently watching his quiet curses assume a misty shape in the cold air, he began to follow the path that led between the garage and the lodge around to the back.

Where the hell was the woman anyway? Cody wondered. He was sure that Pepper had let her friend know that he was coming; she wasn't the type to forget to do something like that. He swore again. If Brooke Kennedy was so damn hostile that she wouldn't even show him a welcoming light or open a door to him, the hell with it!

"Be patient with her, Cody—she's had a rough time."

Pepper's last worried words to him surfaced in his mind, and Cody forced himself to calm down. But, he told himself firmly, if you can't find her, you can hardly help her. The thought cheered him slightly. Maybe she'd gone away for a while. He could take that cruise after all.

As he was rounding a dark corner something hit him squarely in the stomach, driving all the breath out of him in an astonished whoosh, and he folded up neatly before measuring his length backward in the snow.

He lay there for a moment, staring up at the stars and trying to remember if breathing was a voluntary or involuntary action. Voluntary? Maybe he'd better try. . . .

The stars winked out for a second as his paralyzed diaphragm resisted his efforts, then Cody found himself drawing the cold night air into his lungs in relieved gasps. He just lay there and breathed for a moment, then was about to try and get up when a voice reached him out of the darkness.

"Don't move unless you want to hit the ground again. Tell me who you are and what you're doing here."

It was a husky, oddly gruff little voice, unmistakably feminine. And if there was any fear in the warning tone, it was strictly controlled.

The discomfort of lying in the freezing snow and the ache in his middle did nothing to improve Cody's already sour temper. "What the hell did you hit me with?" he demanded, irritated by the wheeze in his voice.

"My feet." It was still a gruff little voice, possessing a faint southern drawl and still containing a warning note. "Shall I demonstrate again?"

Instead of obeying the tone, Cody made a determined effort to gain his feet. "Now, look" he began, and broke off abruptly as he found himself once more sitting in the snow, his feet neatly cut from under him.

"Who are you?" she demanded, still nothing more than a voice out of the darkness.

If his good sense had prevailed, Cody would have sat meekly in the snow and explained who he was. But the culmination of a rough drive up here, a hostile welcome that had painfully deprived him of breath, and the current freezing of his nether regions lost the battle between good sense and recklessness. He surged to his feet, attempting a feint sideways to avoid her obviously skilled defenses.

It wasn't her fault that he misjudged the slippery path and the angle of his dodge, both of which caused his left foot to slide violently to one side and bang painfully against the stone corner of the building. The violence behind that slide also twisted his ankle in a motion it rebelled against, and Cody sank back down on the path with a bitten-off groan as red-hot pain sliced all the way up to his skull.

At least the woman was still and silent, not laughing at him, he thought bitterly. He nursed the injured ankle with both hands and directed his gaze into the blackness out of which her voice had come. "My name is Cody Nash," he told her flatly through gritted teeth. "And if you're Brooke Kennedy, I've come to help you."

There was a moment of silence, then she said calmly, "If that's so, you're a day early; you weren't supposed to arrive until tomorrow."

Cody held on to his ankle and his temper with both hands. "I was warned in Butte that a storm was coming later tonight and advised to get up here while I still could. Satisfied?" he finished coldly.

She apparently wasn't. "Who sent you?"

His exasperated sigh misted in front of his eyes. "Pepper sent me. Right now she's back in Maine with an anxious husband, two dogs, a cat, and possible twins—and, if you ask me, worrying unnecessarily about a friend who can obviously take care of herself!"

A patch of darkness disconnected itself from the rest to kneel in front of him, and Cody cautiously studied the hooded form he could barely make out.

"How's the ankle?" she asked, no hint of apology in her tone.

"Sprained at the very least," he told her bitterly.

She offered a gloved hand. "I'll help you inside."

"Don't put yourself out," he advised with awful politeness.

The hooded form rose abruptly to its feet. "If you want to sit there on your bruised ego and freeze," she told him evenly, "then do it. I'll be sure someone digs you out in the spring."

An angry stab from his ankle and growing numbness made Cody decide to ignore his injured pride. Sighing, he held out a hand. "Sorry," he apologized ironically. "I get this way whenever I'm kicked in the stomach with no warning."

Silently she helped him to his one good foot, her arm going immediately around his waist to steady him on the slippery path. Throwing away the last of his pride, Cody let himself lean on her, his arm around her shoulders. She was strong, which surprised him since the form he was leaning on felt slender to the point of frailness even through her thick coat. She also moved with a cat-footed sureness along the icy path, even with his dot-and-carry movements beside her.

She guided him on around the building to a door that opened—thankfully—directly out onto a flat cement walkway. The door was opened swiftly and he was led inside to find a large and old-fashioned kitchen, its light due entirely to the blazing fire in the huge stone fireplace.

Cody eased himself down in a ladder-back chair by the round oak table, straining his eyes in the dimness to watch her cross the room to a counter. "You like darkness?" he asked.

There was the scrape of a match and then a flickering flame as she lit a large kerosene lantern on the counter. "Power's out," she told him briefly. "And so's the generator. Ice storm yesterday. That's why it was so slippery outside."

She certainly didn't waste words, he thought dryly. A box of matches slid across the table toward him, and before he could catch more than a glimpse of her still-hooded form, she was carrying her lighted lamp toward a second doorway.

"There's another lamp on the table. I'll go find the first-aid box."

Being careful with his throbbing ankle, Cody unfastened his jacket and shrugged out of it, hanging it on the back of another chair nearby. He found the matches and the lantern, even larger than the one she'd lit, trimming the wick and lighting it until the room was fairly bright.

He looked around at the spotless kitchen, the copper pots and pans hanging around a central work island, the colorful Navaho rugs and curtains. With light it was now a cheery room, and the warmth from the fire was beginning to seep into his frozen bones. Cody bent to remove his left boot, grimacing with every movement of the hot, swollen ankle.

Morosely he thought of the sunny cruise he should have been on, making a mental note to get even with Pepper before either of them was much older. He sat back in the surprisingly comfortable chair, listening to the crackle of the fire and the silence and wondering how soon he'd be able to attempt the drive back down. If the storm held off, he decided, he'd try tomorrow—ankle or no ankle. He wasn't about to hang around and try to help this cold woman with her remote voice and her obvious competence at taking care of herself.

She didn't want his help, she obviously didn't need his help and besides, he was becoming more and more convinced that Pepper's worry was due to her pregnancy and little else. He'd tell her that her friend was fine—how, he wondered, had this cold woman won Pepper's warm affection—and then he'd take that cruise after all.

But when Brooke Kennedy came back into the room, his plans shattered like so much brittle ice.

She'd shed the thick coat, revealing a too slender but perfectly curved figure advertised by a thin, ribbed gold turtleneck sweater and faded jeans. Her hair was true black that reflected blue high-lights, and it was at least waist-length. It was pulled tightly away from her face at the moment and gathered high on her head in a ponytail. The style emphasized the striking widow's peak and her marvelous bone structure. Her perfectly formed brows were twin wings above eyes the palest, greenest green Cody could ever remember seeing. High cheekbones, a straight, delicate nose, a mouth designed by nature for kissing and laughter . . .

She was beautiful, Cody thought. Strikingly, stunningly beautiful. And that beautiful, perfect face was as remote as a windswept glacier. The lovely eyes were shuttered and still, the lips, though naturally curved, showed no laughter.

Cody, staring at her and forgetting to breathe, watched as she placed a first-aid box on the table and opened it, seemingly completely unmoved by his steady gaze. He searched the beautiful face for life, and found nothing.

She looked at him. "I know a little first aid. Or would you rather?" She was holding a roll of elastic bandage.

"If you would. Please." He heard his voice and was dimly astonished at its calm tone.

She pulled forward a kitchen step stool and sat down on it, turning up his pant leg and removing the sock before beginning to wind the bandage around his swollen ankle. Her touch was deft, gentle, and totally impersonal.

Acutely aware of the cool touch of her long, graceful fingers, Cody stared at her face and wondered. Beautiful. God, yes, she was beautiful. But that remote coldness, the shuttered eyes . . .

He tried to convince himself that he saw emptiness, that nothing at all lay beneath the perfection of features, but instinct and intuition warned him not to believe that. Empty eyes needed no shutters to hide what they contained. But that remote face . . .

Watching her intently, he only dimly heard a sudden wail as the wind picked up outside, but he saw her reaction. The green eyes slid sideways suddenly, darting quickly toward the outside door.

And for a moment, a single instant, her eyes held stark fear.

It was over almost immediately, and he could almost hear her mind identifying the sound and classifying it as something normal, something unthreatening. The shutters were up again; her fingers completed their task with the remote impersonal touch. She rose after calmly putting his sock back on.

"Coffee?" she asked casually, moving toward the counter and a large thermos there.

"Thanks." What, he wondered, had terrified this woman? Her remoteness, he was now almost certain, was neither innate to her nor indicative of coldness. It was control, he thought; a rigid, fierce control over fear. And something told him that Brooke Kennedy wasn't easily frightened.

He no longer thought Pepper's worry the product of imagination.

She set a cup of steaming liquid in front of him on the table, gesturing wordlessly toward the sugar and cream containers near the lamp, then retreated back to the counter and leaned against it to hold her own cup.

"I tried to stop you from coming," she told him in the distant, oddly gruff voice. "But by the time I got hold of Pepper, you were already on your way."

Cody sipped his coffee slowly as he watched her. He ignored both tone and words to say casually, "You must be a good friend of hers."

He was rewarded for the statement by the first sign of warmth he'd yet seen on her lovely face. There was even a faint, brief spark of humor in her remarkable eyes. "Do you think," she asked dryly, "that anyone could meet Pepper and not become a good friend?"

Cody grinned. "Not a chance! Pepper hugs the world."

Inexplicably the spark vanished as though it had never existed. "Yes," she murmured, then shook her head slightly and abruptly changed the subject. "Sorry about the welcome. I was walking back up from the barn when I heard you coming around the corner. I decided to stack the deck in my favor before asking questions."

He felt his sore stomach ruefully. "Is that what you call it? Stacking the deck in your favor? I thought I'd been hit by a train."

"Karate," she said, his remark winning no spark this time. "Comes in handy sometimes."

Cody nodded, watching her and reaching for another spark. "Is that why you learned first aid? To be able to patch up your victims?"

She looked at him for a long moment. No spark, no visible reaction. Then her eyes slid almost involuntarily toward the door again before returning to his face. Abruptly she said, "You won't be able to drive back down with that ankle. I can take you down in the Sno-Cat; there's a shortcut."

"Anxious to be rid of me?" he drawled softly.

Green eyes reflected the fire's light and nothing else; her voice remained even and remote. Disinterested. "You can report to Pepper that I'm fine, and that I'm sorry I worried her. I have guests coming next week; the lodge is doing great. Then, your duty discharged, you can go on to wherever you'd planned to go before Pepper roped you into this."

Presented with a quick and easy way out of his obligations, Cody was perversely determined not to take advantage of it. "Oh, I think I'll stick around for a few days. This is a guest lodge, right? So consider me a paying guest." As she opened her mouth to speak he added smoothly, "At least until the ankle heals."

Instead of speaking immediately, she sipped her coffee for a moment. When she finally did respond to his statement, he could have sworn that there was a note of relief in her voice. "Am I going to be faced with a lawsuit, Mr. Nash?"

"Cody." He smiled slowly. "Of course not. Why would I sue you? Just because I slipped on an icy path and loused up my ankle? Going to court is no way to start a . . . friendship."

Quite suddenly she laughed. And it startled Cody in more ways than one. It was an oddly musical laugh, catching one by surprise after the soft gruffness of her speaking voice. And it was puzzling because the amusement in her voice never reached her eyes. In fact, the riveting green orbs held more than a touch of bitterness.

"Pepper didn't warn you about me, did she?"

"Warn me?" he probed cautiously.

"She didn't." Brooke raised her coffee cup in a slightly mocking toast. "Here's to Pepper and her tact. I wonder if she realized I'd tell you myself."

"Tell me what?" Cody asked warily.

Brooke Kennedy threw the answer at him as if it were a gauntlet, a challenge she didn't expect him to take up. She flung it at him in the tone of a woman who was braced for a reaction she'd seen one too many times.

"I read minds, Mr. Nash. I'm a certified, bona fide psychic."

"Really?" Cody leaned forward, both his tone and his posture that of keen interest. "That's fascinating. All minds, or just some? Can you read my mind?"

Green eyes flickered in a surprise nothing short

of astonishment and then dropped as she sipped her coffee again.

Cody silently congratulated himself. It didn't take a genius to realize what kind of reaction she was accustomed to after that statement: wariness, mistrust, even fear. He was thankful that she wasn't the first psychic he'd encountered, thankful that he was aware of the problems she'd probably gone through because of her gift. He realized then that her rigid control guarded more than just fear.

"You didn't answer me," he prodded softly.

She looked back at him, the shutters down for a brief moment and uncertainty peeking out. Then, with the control probably built up over a lifetime of being a target for suspicion, she was shut inside herself again. "To the first question: I don't know; I haven't encountered 'all minds.' To the second question: I don't know; I haven't tried."

"You have to try?" he asked, honestly interested. "I mean, d'you have to concentrate?"

Brooke nodded a bit jerkily. "I do now. I learned to—to build a wall. I had to."

"I'm sorry," he said very quietly.

"You're . . . sorry?" Her tone was surprised, wondering.

Cody felt a sudden surge of rage so strong that he had to swallow hard before he could even speak. Lord, had no one ever shown compassion for this woman? he asked himself. Was she convinced that no one would understand what it meant to be locked away inside herself? "I'm sorry . . . because walls are lonely things. I'm sorry you had to build one."

A slight frown drew her flying brows together as she studied him, a frown of uncertainty and confusion. Then she shook her head. "You're an unusual man, Mr. Nash," she said almost inaudibly.

"Cody," he repeated gently, patiently.

After a moment she murmured, "Cody, then."

"May I return the favor?" he asked, still gentle.

She nodded slightly, but said nothing.

He studied her, a frown beginning to draw his own brows together. Cody had met few women toward whom he felt any protective impulses, probably because he'd come of age during the women's movement and had tried to respect everything that it stood for. But instincts and impulses were stirring to life now; he felt an almost overwhelming urge to protect Brooke Kennedy.

But from what?

She was afraid of something or someone, and the control she'd built up couldn't stand against that fear. He could have asked her point-blank, but knew that she wouldn't tell him. Not yet anyway. Cody had the feeling that Brooke didn't trust easily. That the lack of trust was all bound up in her psychic abilities he didn't doubt; it made his self-imposed task more difficult. For her to trust him, she'd have to open up, and he couldn't help but wonder if years behind her wall had destroyed that ability.

Two

Brooke felt his searching stare, and she didn't need ESP to realize that Cody had made some sort of decision. This golden man, she thought, had decided to stay here for a while.

She felt stiff, uncomfortable with that realization. She'd always been more nervous around men, and the compassion in this man's eyes unnerved her even more. At the same time she was glad he would be around tonight; she was afraid to be alone tonight.

Hurt . . .

Setting her coffee cup aside and instantly regaining control of the tremor that shook her hand, she asked him calmly, "Have you eaten? I have a small butane stove, and I was planning to fix an omelet."

Cody, who'd seen the tremor, bit back a question. "I had something in Butte, but that was hours ago. If it wouldn't be too much trouble . . ."

"Of course not." Brooke was already getting the small stove out of the closet near the back door, silently fighting to keep her concentration at full strength.

"I'd offer to help," Cody said wryly, "but—"

"I think I can manage." Her mind only half on his response, Brooke wasn't conscious of her abrupt tone.

Cody felt his fingers beginning to drum rhythmically on the table and quickly stopped them. He told himself to be patient, to go slowly unless he wanted to put her even more on-guard than she already was. But the remoteness of her voice cut at him. He searched his mind for some casual conversation, something to help her relax.

"Do you live up here all alone?" he asked finally.

"When there are no guests, yes. Except for Mister, that is."

"Who's Mister?"

"He's a burro." Brooke went to the refrigerator for the ingredients for the omelets. "He was my uncle's . . . pet."

"But not yours?" Cody gathered that she spoke of the uncle who'd left her this lodge.

Breaking eggs into a large bowl, Brooke sent him a quick glance, feeling a faint prickle of humor. "Not exactly. Mister's almost as old as I am. He's nearsighted, bad-tempered, and hates every living thing now that my uncle Josh is gone."

"Is he the reason you were at the barn when I arrived?" Cody asked easily, determined to keep alive that spark of amusement he'd seen.

She nodded. "With weather like the kind we've been having these last few weeks, he prefers his stable to the pasture. I was down there feeding him."

After a moment of silence broken only by the crackle of the fire and the slight sounds she made cooking, Cody tried again. He was beginning to feel like a salmon swimming upstream.

"How often do you have guests up here? Is there a definite season?"

"No real season. I usually have a group stay four or five times a year, mostly during the summer."

"No more often than that?" He shook his head slightly. "You're up here alone the rest of the time?"

"I'm used to being alone."

Her words had been easy, her voice still remote, and Cody felt a sharp stab of compassion. Lord, but she had a right to be bitter! He wondered if she guarded her mind even while alone, and knew somehow that she did. Could she never allow herself to relax?

Caution went by the board.

"I'll bet you weren't alone before you learned to shut out everyone else's thoughts," he said probingly.

Brooke tipped the first omelet onto a plate and carried it and a handful of silverware over to the table. She set the plate in front of him, looking at his inquiring expression with nothing at all on her own face. When she spoke, it seemed as if she'd gone off on a tangent.

"Have you ever been around others and thought something which was, let's say, unkind? A thought that never made it to speech because of innate good manners or tact?"

"Sure." Cody frowned a little. "I'm sure we've all done that."

She nodded. "But we don't speak, because thoughts put into words can never be taken back."

"True."

"Before I learned to build a wall," she told him tonelessly, "I heard those thoughts. All of them. The petty jealousies, the cruelties, the insults never voiced. Even the unconscious thoughts that would horrify if one were aware of them."

Cody stared up into the remarkable green eyes, and what he felt in that moment he couldn't define. "I'm sorry, Brooke," he said huskily.

She looked at him for a moment. "Your omelet's getting cold." Then she turned and went back to the small stove on the counter.

Silently he dug in. After a moment, watching as she prepared her own meal, he said, "You're a good cook."

"Thanks."

Cody reached desperately for normality. "Did your mother teach you?"

Brooke sat down across the table from him with her own plate, and in the flickering light, he saw pain and bitterness flash in her eyes briefly before the shutters closed.

"No," she said flatly.

He realized then that he couldn't expect normality, and Cody wasn't one to strive for what wasn't there. There were murky waters to get through before he could expect to know this woman. He wanted to know her. *Had* to know her.

"Here there be dragons," he said softly.

Brooke looked at him sharply. "What?"

Cody's eyes were hooded, watchful. "Think back to history classes in school. Remember those old maps of the world when it was mostly uncharted?" He didn't wait for a response, but went on in a musing voice. "The continents were weird shapes and all squashed together; a lot was missing. And at the edges of the unknown, unexplored territory were the words *Here there be dragons*."

She shook her head. "You've lost me."

"It's a problem in getting to know someone." He kept his voice easy. "You say something casual, maybe just making conversation, and touch a nerve without meaning to. You suddenly find yourself teetering on the edge of a pit, an area of darkness not to be probed. . . . Here there be dragons."

He continued to watch her, but Brooke returned his gaze without expression or comment. After a moment Cody shrugged slightly.

"When that happens, you have two choices. You can back off; catch your balance, retreat to safer ground. Explored territory."

"Or?" Brooke asked evenly.

"Or"—he smiled crookedly—"if you're an inquisitive soul, an explorer, you ignore the warning and step off into the pit. Launch yourself into those uncharted areas and battle the dragons. Or prove they don't exist."

Brooke looked down and concentrated on her food. "And so?"

"And so"—he took a deep breath—"tell me about your mother."

"I see you're a dragonslayer," she said without looking up, striving to keep her voice casual.

"Looks that way, doesn't it?"

"Don't try to slay my dragons, Cody," she told him very quietly. "They're the fire-breathing kind. You'll get burned."

Those statements caused Cody to chalk up several points in her favor. Because she was quick enough to understand exactly what he'd meant; because she was honest enough not to pretend that she hadn't understood; and because she was clearly warning him to turn his damn boat back around and get out of those uncharted seas.

The lady was a challenge.

Lightly he said, "I'll wear an asbestos suit."

"You'll be burned to a cinder."

"I'll bring along a fire extinguisher."

"Ineffective against a dragon's fiery breath."

Delighted with the humor, Cody said sadly, "Better men than I have tried before, eh?"

A faint flush rose in her cheeks, and Brooke shot a wry glance at him. "No," she murmured.

"No?" he probed in surprise.

She hesitated, wondering irritably why she was telling him this. "I've always avoided—uh—relationships. For some reason ESP tends to frighten men more than women."

"You mean, you're—"

"Yes," she muttered.

Cody was honestly astonished. "How old are you?"

"Twenty-eight."

He stared across the table at the most beautiful woman he'd ever seen and wondered briefly how many total idiots one woman could encounter in her lifetime. "Then the men you've known have been morons," he told her calmly.

She laughed in spite of herself, looking up just in time to see the intent way he was looking at her. Trying to ignore the warmth of his golden eyes, she said reasonably, "You can't blame them. It must be very unsettling to find out that the lady can read your mind."

"Doesn't unsettle me," Cody said firmly, wondering how to extract that musical laugh more often.

"So you say." Brooke kept eating, feeling more relaxed now because only the wind was howling outside. Nothing else. It was gone again.

Cody finished his own omelet and sipped his coffee. "I don't mean this to sound crass," he said carefully, "but when did you confide your ESP to these moronic gentlemen?"

Brooke laughed again at the careful phrasing. "D'you mean, at what stage of the game did they back off?" she asked wryly.

There was an answering twinkle in the golden eyes meeting hers. "I was trying to be delicate," Cody said reprovingly.

"Mmm." She lifted a brow at him. "Well, I'll be blunt. The gentlemen were told at a very early stage; I thought it was only fair that they be warned."

"Is that why you told me right off the bat?" he asked softly.

The question caught Brooke off-guard, and she stared across at him, her mind moving in slow motion. Was that really why she'd told him? Had that instant and confusing awareness of a stranger caused her to employ the weapon of her abilities so quickly? Had a deeply buried, little-used feminine instinct warned her that this man could hurt her?

She looked down at her plate. "Don't be ridiculous. You're a stranger. I—"

He reached across the table to cover one of her hands with his. "Don't. Don't run away from me." His voice was very deep.

Brooke stared at the strong brown hand covering hers for a long moment, her gaze finally lifting to his face. "You're a stranger," she repeated steadily.

"I don't feel like a stranger."

"But you are."

His hand tightened on hers. "Brooke, I know what's in all the unwritten rule books. I know that in relationships one step follows another—usually slowly. But I feel as if we've skipped a few steps. I came in here intending to leave as soon as possible. I'm being honest, you see. Then I met a fascinating lady—and it'll take more willpower than I've got to make me leave."

Brooke sat back abruptly, pulling her hand from beneath his. "D'you usually get results with that line?" she asked in a brittle voice.

Quietly he said, "That was a cheap shot."

"Was it?" She refused to meet his eyes. "Yes, I suppose it was. You'll have to forgive me; I seem to have forgotten the rules."

There was a long silence then Cody began speaking in a calm, level tone.

"I'm thirty-five years old, single, a Scorpio if that matters. I work as a free-lance troubleshooter in computers—which just means that I travel from one company to another and untangle someone else's problems. I was born and raised in Texas, and both my parents and my younger sister live there; I have an apartment in Virginia in which I seldom stay since I generally live out of a suitcase."

Brooke was looking at him now, puzzled and wary. "I don't—"

He cut her off, still calm, dispassionate. "I enjoy chess, poker, and jigsaw puzzles. I read mysteries and science-fiction. I'm a licensed pilot. My favorite colors are green and burgundy. I don't bite my nails or snore. I'm a pretty fair cook, a first-rate dishwasher, and I was taught to put away my clothing neatly."

Brooke was beginning to smile.

Satisfied, Cody kept going. "Since college, I've been gainfully employed in a job that pays exorbitant fees, so I've managed to salt away quite a bit for a rainy day. I've also been involved in at least two serious relationships. The first ended when I discovered that my fourth-grade English teacher was married to a fellow bearing a close resemblance to a Mack truck. The second ended some years later, mainly due to a conflict of careers . . . and of personalities.

"Since then, I have—in the popular vernacular—dated occasionally. Nothing serious, because I'm never in one place long enough. I'm by no means avoiding matrimony, since I happen to believe it's a dandy institution. In fact, I'd love an ivy-covered cottage, two-point-five kids, a mongrel dog, and a snooty cat. And a wife. The possibility of the latter, in fact, has been on my mind quite a bit lately."

"How lately?" she murmured.

Cody pushed back the sleeve of his flannel shirt and looked rather pointedly at his watch. "Since a little less than two hours ago," he told her, totally deadpan.

Brooke was still smiling. "It'd never work," she said gravely.

"Why not?"

"I'm a Scorpio too." She shook her head. "Dragons are bad enough, but it you put two Scorpios in the same boat, there's going to be a hell of a storm."

"I think we can weather it."

"I think you're crazy."

"Not at all." Conversationally he added, "I very much think I'm falling in love with you, you see. And love seems to make improbabilities turn into definite possibilities."

Brooke stopped smiling. She gazed across the oak table into golden eyes, and the calm conviction there stole her breath. "Now I know you're crazy," she said almost inaudibly.

Soberly Cody said, "I almost wish I were.

Because something tells me you were right about that storm. After thirty-five relatively blameless years, I had to go and fall for a woman who first kicks me in the stomach and then warns me to stay the hell away from her dragons. You never did tell me about your mother, you know."

She ignored that last. "You can't fall in love with a stranger," she told him tightly.

"Don't tell me that I can't do what I am doing," he said quietly.

Brooke felt an almost overwhelming urge to burst into tears, and it shook her as she hadn't been shaken by anything in a long time. "Don't," she murmured. "Don't say that. You don't know . . . what it means. You don't know what I am. . . ."

Softly insistent, he said, "I know you're a beautiful, intelligent woman who's hidden herself away somewhere. I know that you've held yourself under rigid control for so long that something has to give."

"I'm a freak!" she burst out suddenly, that "something" finally giving way with an explosive sound. "Something unnatural to be stared at, and pointed at, and tested, and examined! Something to be afraid of because it isn't normal! Something to hide and be ashamed of, something to put in a closet or in a sideshow—"

Her voice broke off in pain and bitterness, and Brooke covered her face with her hands, trying desperately to regain the control that had splintered. And she might have been able to regain it, might have been able to hide herself away again. Except for Cody.

He rose and came around to her chair, automatically careful of his injured ankle as he leaned back against the table and grasped her upper arms, drawing her to her feet.

Blindly Brooke fought to pull away from him. "No," she said unsteadily. "No, don't be kind—"

"It isn't kindness, dammit," he muttered roughly, ignoring her efforts and pulling her firmly against him. His arms went around her and held her tightly. "It isn't kindness."

Brooke fought against the wrenching, tearing need to cry. But the tears were dragged up from some well deep within herself, pulled inexorably by the gentleness of his touch, his soothing, wordless murmur. She'd never known such compassion and understanding from a man; her father had died when she was very young, and her uncle Josh had been a brisk, undemonstrative man.

She was tired from too many sleepless nights, bitter with years of memory, frightened by something she didn't understand, and shaken by Cody's declaration of falling in love with her. The haven of his arms was too powerful to resist.

Cody held her tightly, still astonished by the depth of what he felt but not bothering to deny it. He'd never thought that love would be something that would creep up behind him and then knock him off his feet in a single blinding instant, but that was what had happened. And he didn't deceive himself into thinking that it was going to be easy.

The woman in his arms, crying with the jerky, shuddering sobs of someone who hadn't let herself cry enough in her life, was complex and wary and unwilling to love easily. Her gift, he thought, had been her curse, and the hurt and bitterness of that went deep.

He was nowhere near having all the answers, but Cody thought that he could guess a few of them. And his heart ached for the little girl who'd been the object of stares and whispers, who'd "heard" thoughts even a hardened adult would have been shocked by. A little girl who'd grown up knowing that she was different, and that people were afraid of her.

And he ached even more for the woman who'd hidden herself away in this valley, allowing only rare and carefully spaced human contact for herself, cultivating a rigid control until it had very nearly drained the life out of her.

As to why she was afraid, he couldn't even begin to guess. He meant to find out; until then he wouldn't leave her alone a moment longer than he had to. He'd stay with her and try to shield her from whatever had stirred the stark terror in her eyes.

Brooke was too bewildered and uncertain of her rampaging emotions to fully give in to them. One by one she drew in the threads of control and pulled them tight until the sobs could be choked off. The unfamiliar hardness of Cody's lean body unnerved her, and she could feel her heart thudding erratically against her ribs. She had to stop this insanity and get away from him, she told herself, before . . . before . . . before he made her feel—

She broke away from the incompleted thought and his arms in the same moment. Turning her back to him, she rubbed the sleeve of her sweater, childlike, across her wet eyes and spoke huskily.

"Well . . . you've certainly had an interesting evening. First you drive up an icy mountain road, then you're kicked in the stomach and sprain your ankle, and then a crazy woman with ESP cries all over you. If you had any sense, you'd just shake hands politely and say, 'Gee, it's been really strange knowing you,' and then run like hell."

Cody chuckled softly, but his golden eyes were

steady and gentle when she turned to look at him hesitantly. "I also started falling in love," he said. "And I'm not about to run."

"Stop saying that!" she ordered almost frantically, nothing at all remote about her face or voice now.

"It's true."

Brooke got a grip on herself. "Look, it's late. I'll go out and get your suitcase—I assume you brought one—and then show you which room is yours. It's been a long day. I'm sure you're tired. I'm tired." She realized that she was talking too quickly, and immediately shut down the flow, adding carefully, "All right?"

He nodded. "All right. My case is in the Jeep out front."

Not trusting herself to say anything more, Brooke merely nodded in response. She picked up the lamp from the counter and headed for the doorway leading to the rest of the house.

Immediately Cody picked up the lamp from the table and, pausing only to throw his jacket over his arm and pick up his boot, followed her. Bound, his ankle could stand a little weight, but Cody nonetheless moved gingerly as he went through the doorway and down a long hall.

Halfway down the hall an archway on the right opened into a huge sunken room the size of an average house. He could barely discern its size and had no idea of the furnishings because of the darkness. Two closed doors were on the left side of the hall, and he didn't bother to open them. He moved instead toward the end of the hall and the glow of Brooke's lamp.

She had set her lamp on a long table near the front door and shrugged into the quilted hooded coat he'd first seen her in. She looked back over her shoulder before opening the door, and for a moment he thought that he saw the fear in her eyes. Then she'd opened the door and headed out for the Jeep.

She left the door open.

Within moments she was back, closing the front door and removing her coat silently. Holding his case, she picked up her lamp again and motioned toward another hallway leading off to the left of the front door.

"Two of the downstairs bedrooms have kerosene heaters and fireplaces," she murmured. "The fires are already banked for the night, but the heaters are on. This way."

The room she showed him to a moment later was as warm as the kitchen; the banked fire in the stone hearth was glowing and the heater was whirring softly. There were bookshelves lining one wall, and a high double bed, sturdy furniture, and bright rugs on the hardwood floor. An old rolltop desk sat in the corner by one window.

Cody knew instinctively that this had been her uncle's room. He set his lamp down on a low chest by the door, watching as she set his case down and stepped quickly back out into the hallway.

"If—if you need anything," she began awkwardly.

He caught her wrist gently. "Will you be all right alone?" he asked.

She looked up at him. "I told you. I'm used to being alone."

His hand released her wrist, lifting to cup her cheek warmly. "You'll have to get used to *not* being alone," he said.

Brooke swallowed hard as the tingling touch of his hand brought a flush to her face. "Good night," she said hastily, turning away.

Cody watched the light from her lamp fade away

into the darkness. After a moment he quietly shut the door.

For the first time in more than a week Brooke slept well. She realized that it was because of Cody's presence, because she wasn't totally alone in the huge lodge, but she didn't care to examine that too closely. Being alone had become an acceptable, if lonely, way of life.

God knew, it was better than being the focus of nervous, wary eyes. . . .

Brooke shoved that thought into a compartment of her mind as she slid out of her bed the next morning. Weak sunlight filtered through the crack in the closed drapes and cast a dim beam across her bedroom; when the drapes were opened a moment later, the cheery room immediately flaunted its bright orange and rust color scheme and lost its murky shadows.

The room was large and comfortable, the furnishings—like most of those in the lodge—were of sturdy oak. Braided rugs brightened the gleaming hardwood floor and the sheer panels behind the drapes allowed lots of light.

Brooke automatically built a fire in the stone fireplace, a bit puzzled by the warmth of the room since she'd cut her kerosene heater off before going to bed. She'd just straightened from the hearth when she heard the furnace come on, and that puzzled her even more. The generator was out. Or at least it had been out last night. And the power lines from town couldn't have been repaired so quickly. What on earth . . . ?

Cody?

Hastily she stepped into the adjoining bathroom and went through her morning ritual of waking up and getting ready to face another day. Then she donned jeans and a bulky knit bright green sweater, warm socks, and loafers. She left her hair hanging straight and gleaming and, except for a moisturizer to combat the dry winter air, wore no makeup.

A glance at the windup clock on her nightstand hurried her steps as she left the bedroom; it was almost ten A.M.

Passing Cody's bedroom, she noted that it was empty and neat. Where was he? Quickly she made her way through the silent house to the kitchen. The tantalizing aroma of coffee pleased her senses in the warm, cheery room, and Brooke paused for a moment to note the freshly built fire in the hearth and the merrily bubbling coffee on her little butane stove.

So he'd made the coffee before the generator was fixed? Experimentally she reached for a light switch. Plenty of juice for the lights and furnace anyway, she realized. Turning the unnecessary light back off, she poured out a cup of coffee and leaned against the counter, sipping it.

Granted a little time for thought, Brooke thought. She felt refreshed and calm after the much needed sleep, and blissfully free of the fear that haunted her at night. Tentatively she reached out, sensing. No. No, it was gone. It was always gone during the day. Only at night—

Something slipped casually into the fringes of her exploring probe. Cody. He was in the barn, making friends with Mister. He was—

Swiftly she pulled the probe back into her mind, frowning a little. Odd, that. She usually had to concentrate hard to sense a stranger. Why had it come so easily with him? Brooke frowned harder. She'd have to watch her guard with Cody Nash.

Remembering the night before, she felt a flush rise in her cheeks. Lord, what must he be thinking? Cried all over by a hysterical woman . . . Brooke shook her head a little ruefully. He'd think she had a split personality in addition to her other weirdnesses when he discovered a totally different woman facing him today!

After nearly three years of exposure to Pepper's crazy friends, Brooke knew that her years of firm control were mostly a thing of the past. She could block out thoughts more without being stiff, and she usually enjoyed the contact with guests here at the lodge.

A kind of acceptance of her abilities had bred relaxation, even amusement. It had begun with a friend she met through Pepper, who had called Brooke in a panic and asked if she would use her ESP to find a lost child who'd wandered away during a camping trip. Doubtful, but wanting desperately to find the child, Brooke had reached out. And the little girl had been located within an hour.

Wary of publicity, Brooke had nonetheless helped other friends periodically. For the first time in her life a sense of her own worth grew out of her abilities, and she'd begun to hope tentatively that they would one day be a blessing instead of a curse.

Still. . . . She thought of the night before with another frown. The bitterness of those early years was still with her; the floodgates had burst with Cody's gentle probing, and with the fear that had made her nervous and uneasy. She had never really come to terms with those early years, Brooke realized. Memory still had the power to hurt her.

She wondered if Cody knew how much he'd unsettled her. She wasn't used to meeting with compassion in strangers—particularly men. Few people casually met were unthreatened by her abilities. Only her friends—mostly unique people she'd met through Pepper—accepted her ESP without a blink. Those friends didn't know of the early years and the bitter seeds sown, which was fine with Brooke; their easy acceptance helped her put everything in perspective.

And so her painful words to Cody the night before had shocked her; she hadn't realized that she still felt that unhappiness so strongly. Had Cody's declaration of love frightened her so badly that she'd reached back into bitter memory for something to shove between them?

Brooke swallowed the last of her coffee and immediately poured another cup. Love? The man was mad. Who would want to get involved with a woman who read minds and possessed dragons? That last brought a crooked smile to her lips. Dragons? Yes, and he'd neatly pounced on the biggest, most fire-breathing dragon of them all. A quick-witted, intelligent man, Brooke thought. And sensitive too. But she wasn't about to get involved with him. Relationships between men and women had too many strikes against them to begin with without throwing ESP into the pot.

So. She'd try her damnedest to prove to him that there was absolutely nothing wrong. She was fine. And then he'd leave.

Brooke felt a sharp pang, and instantly squashed it. He'd leave. If she could only get him away from here before night and the fear came— he'd leave. And she'd face that bogey in the dark the best way she could.

She looked up quickly when the back door swung inward, not surprised by his entrance because she'd felt him coming. Almost absently she shored up her walls to guard against his odd ability to creep into her mind.

"Morning." Cody brushed snow off his shoulders, bright golden eyes looking at her intently.

"Morning." Brooke forced down the thought that last night's lamplight hadn't done him justice; how many hearts had he broken with those incredible golden eyes? Her eyes skimmed over his broad shoulders, the leanly muscular frame, then back up unconsciously to examine a face that was very nearly classical in its masculine beauty. A golden man, she thought dimly, with all the warmth and compelling attraction of the precious metal that had built kingdoms and toppled them.

Gold fever, she thought, and then hastily dismissed the implications of that. "You've been busy, I see. How's the ankle?"

Cody was so fascinated by the easy amusement in her green eyes and the warmth in that gruff little voice that he nearly forgot to answer. "Oh, it's better. The swelling's gone down quite a bit. I've been making friends with Mister—although the effort was somewhat one-sided."

Brooke started to tell him that she knew exactly where he'd been, but swallowed the words. And she realized that last night's declaration wasn't going to be referred to; Cody apparently understood that she was hardly ready for love from a stranger. She said, "I gather you've also been fixing the generator."

He shrugged out of his jacket and crossed the room to hang it on the back of a kitchen chair, limping only slightly. "It wasn't hard. I scrounged a bit and found some spare parts in the shed with the generator. Besides, I thought we'd probably need the juice; there's a blizzard starting up out there."

She turned to look out the window, a little surprised to realize that she hadn't thought to check the weather before. She saw snow beginning to blow around outside, the flakes ominously large. Absently she said, "I wonder why last night's storm never hit; it looks like it was holding back until today."

"Stranded for days."

"I can always take you down in the Sno-Cat." Brooke turned away from the window and looked at Cody, only vaguely noting his startled expression. "The Cat can get through anything."

Cody stared at her for a long moment. "How about some breakfast first?"

Brooke felt herself flush. She wondered if Cody understood why she was trying to send him on his way. Would that startle him? "Sorry. I guess I'm being a bad hostess. What would you like?"

"Whatever you're having." Cody eased his weight down into a chair, watching her and still wearing a bemused expression.

Brooke turned away again and busied herself with preparing breakfast. Anything to avoid thinking about how right he looked in her home.

"Do you cook when you have guests?"

"I help." With her back still to him, she began mixing pancake batter. "There's a lady in town who comes up when I have guests. She's a retired cook, and enjoys keeping her hand in occasionally."

"Do you like music?"

Amused at the leapfrogging subjects, Brooke asked, "What is this, Twenty Questions?"

"Humor me."

"I love music."

"Animals?"

"Yes, although I haven't been around them much."

"Where were you born?"

"Alabama. Next question?" she asked wryly,

carefully pouring the batter onto the heated griddle.

"What do you like to read?"

"Murder mysteries, intrigue, and science fiction."

"Do you realize you've been reading my mind?"

Three

Brooke set the mixing bowl down on the counter with exaggerated care and slowly turned to look at him. He was sitting by the table, one elbow resting on its polished surface and his hand cupping his chin. The golden eyes were still a bit bemused, but steady.

She realized then that only the sound of her own voice had disturbed the silence between them. Cody hadn't said a word aloud since he'd told her that he would have whatever she was having for breakfast.

"I'm sorry," she whispered, horrified.

Philosophically Cody said, "That's the damned-est thing I ever saw. Or heard. Whatever. At least I'll never have to worry about holding up my end of a conversation with you, will I?"

Hardly hearing him, Brooke lifted a hand to rub

her forehead fretfully. "That shouldn't have happened," she muttered. "How did that happen?"

"It jarred me at first," Cody said, musingly. "You said something about the storm waiting to hit today and I thought, stranded for days. It was a delighted thought, by the way. Then you said you could take me down in the Sno-Cat, and I realized you'd read the thought. The rest was—uh—an experiment."

Shaken by the slip in her control, Brooke snapped, "That was a sneaky trick!"

"I know." He was disarmingly rueful. "But I wanted to know if you could read me, and I had a feeling you wouldn't try if I'd asked."

"I wouldn't have." Brooke turned back to the griddle and flipped the pancakes over. "Don't—don't do that again, Cody."

"I won't." There was a pause, then he asked softly, "Forgive me?"

Irritably she said, "If your ankle was strong enough to carry you down to the barn, it's strong enough to move around the kitchen. There's orange juice in the refrigerator and the plates are in that cabinet."

"Yes, ma'am." Amused, Cody got up and began to set the table. A moment later he said conversationally, "It doesn't bother me if you read my mind, you know."

"It bothers *me*," she said briefly.

"Why?" he asked, honestly interested.

Brooke turned the strips of bacon sizzling in the pan, trying to think of some way to explain the inexplicable. "It just bothers me. Look, it's very disconcerting to have someone else's thought running through my mind."

"I'd think you'd be used to it by now."

"I'll never get used to it."

"Which is why you live way up here like a hermit?"

She looked back over her shoulder at him, surprised by the touch of anger in his voice. "I cope the best way I can," she told him tightly.

"By hiding away from the problem?"

She carried the pancakes and bacon over to the table, his accusation getting to her in spite of herself. "Don't lay that on me," she snapped. "You don't know the whole story."

"Then tell me," he invited instantly.

Brooke set the plate down and glared across the table at him. "No!"

"I can't fight the dragons until I can see them."

"You're not going to fight anything."

"Brooke—"

"I'll take you back to town after breakfast. The Cat can—"

"The hell you will," he interrupted flatly. "I'm not going anywhere, Brooke."

"I'll call the police and have you thrown out," she said desperately, filled with the strong conviction that unless she got him out of her life immediately, she'd no longer be in control. And she'd fought too long and too hard for control to lose it willingly.

"You can't call them," he taunted softly. "The phone's out; I tried it this morning."

"Then I'll go to town myself in the Cat, and—"

He interrupted again. "If I could fix a generator, I could damn well disable a Sno-Cat."

Brooke stared at him.

"You're stuck with me." His voice was still soft, but no longer taunting, his gaze level and calm. "And I've waited too long just to walk away because of a few lousy dragons."

"Waited?" She had the uneasy feeling that his

silence on a certain unnerving subject was about to be broken. And she was right.

"For love," he said simply.

"You don't love me, Cody." Brooke put every ounce of certainty she could muster into the words. "Because you don't know me. Maybe you think you're in love, but you aren't. Love at first sight's a myth. It—"

"It wasn't at first sight," Cody said calmly. "It took a few minutes."

She ignored that. "You can't love someone without knowing them, and you don't know me! My God—we only met last night!"

"Brooke, stop telling me that I can't feel what I feel."

She tried another tack. "Well, I'm sorry, but I don't feel what you think you feel." Brooke felt a wild giggle trying to rise in her throat. Had that sentence been right? It hadn't sounded right. Seeing that Cody was coming around the table to her, she added hastily, "And I won't ever feel that way. Ever. So you'd better just go."

Cody's grin was honestly amused, but there was a glint in his eyes. "The lady's protesting awfully loud," he noted, halting barely an arm's length away from her.

Brooke refused to back away from him physically. She lifted her chin and stared defiantly into the lazily smiling eyes. "If nothing else, the lady certainly knows her own mind. I'm not protesting, Cody. I'm stating a fact. And the fact is that I'm not interested. Period."

The next thing she knew, Brooke found herself hauled against his chest and locked in an embrace that was inescapable without being painful. Even through her sweater and his, she could feel his heart thudding against her in a rapid and erratic rhythm.

"This is the second time I've held you," he said huskily. "But this time, I'm afraid I don't feel at all protective—or soothing."

"Cody!" She pushed against his chest, disconcerted by the way her senses flared at the contact with unyielding muscles. But then her senses overloaded in a burst of inner sparks as his mouth found hers.

Brooke was hardly sweet-twenty-eight-and-never-been-kissed. There had been tentative beginnings during the last couple of years. But as she'd told Cody, it must have been very nerve-racking to discover that the lady could read minds; those tentative beginnings had remained only beginnings. Experience of sorts.

But she had never in her life felt anything like this. The sensory overload was frightening and yet strangely, insidiously addictive. She felt blind, deaf, and mute—aware only of sensations exploding inside her too rapidly to be assimilated.

She felt one of his hands tangle in her long hair, felt the other hand slide down to the small of her back and draw her impossibly closer. Warm lips moved demandingly on hers, taking with a fierce hunger that wouldn't be denied. His tongue probed in the stark thrust of possession, igniting a fire that swept through Brooke in a raging, out-of-control blaze.

When Cody finally lifted his head, Brooke had to force her eyes to open. With a dim, wondering sort of surprise she saw that her arms were up around his neck, her fingers locked in his thick golden hair. She told her fingers to let go, her arms to fall to her sides. Nothing happened. His voice distracted her from vague annoyance.

"Time isn't important," Cody said hoarsely, golden eyes darkened to honey as he stared down at her. "Depth is. I may not know you with my mind yet, but I know you with my heart. And I've caught a glimpse of those dragons, Brooke. I'll find them and slay them, or I'll prove that they can't hurt you anymore. And I'll know you with my mind."

In a split second of understanding, Brooke realized why she'd felt threatened almost from the first moment she'd laid eyes on Cody: She'd known with some instinct beyond knowledge that this man could step inside her walls and, once inside, see her in a way she'd never been seen before. And the Brooke who'd searched most of her life for privacy and found it at last marching hand in hand with loneliness felt a tug-of-war beginning inside of her.

She needed her privacy as balm for those bitter early years; at the same time what Cody was offering was almost irresistible. Offering? No. What he was *demanding*. It was almost irresistible, and scary as hell. He wanted to see her with walls down, wanted to see the parts of her hiding from the light.

Brooke, who'd seen quite a few psychologists and parapsychologists in her time, knew what that was called: psychological visibility. It was a basic need of human beings, according to the theory, to be clearly seen by at least one other person.

That was what Cody demanded as a lover's right.

And that scared the hell out of Brooke, because in all the years of seeing into other people's minds, no one had yet looked into her own.

This time her arms and hands obeyed her silent commands, and Brooke stepped back away from Cody. She broke the lock of his intense gaze, glancing down at the table. "The food's cold," she said in a faraway voice. "I'll put it in the microwave."

"Brooke."

She picked the plate up before meeting his eyes. And her own was naked now, shutters unable to stand against him. She wasn't sure that the walls would be able to either, and that fear was reflected in green depths.

Cody swore softly. "Brooke, don't look at me like that," he said, and there was a rough note of pleading in his tone. "I won't batter my way through those walls of yours, if that's what you're afraid of. I wouldn't hurt you like that. All I'm asking for is time. Time to find out if you can meet me halfway. That's all—I promise."

Brooke tried to ignore the pleading, and found it one of the hardest things she'd ever done in her life. "You're asking too much. And you're moving too fast."

"I'll slow down," he promised instantly.

She looked into his eyes, startled, wondering at the intensity he seemed to feel so clearly. Did it matter so much to him? *Was* he really in love with her?

A seed buried deep inside of her began to grow in that moment. Tentatively, afraid of its own vulnerability, it began to reach out for the warm light of hope.

She was so tired of being alone.

Nodding jerkily, Brooke turned away and toward the countertop microwave oven. "Better unpack your asbestos suit," she warned shakily. "I think you just might need it."

They shared the cleaning-up chores in a companionable silence broken only by desultory conversation. Their words were meaningless, unimportant, but the very casualness of them helped to relax two wary people. Afterward Brooke showed Cody the lodge.

The enormous place contained six bedrooms upstairs in addition to the two downstairs, four bathrooms, a large formal dining room, and—the room Cody had noticed the night before—a sunken great room.

It was this room they wound up in. It was huge. At the front of the room was a tremendous stone fireplace with a raised hearth, before which lay an ankle-deep, snow-white polar bearskin rug. Synthetic, Brooke explained, since her uncle hadn't believed in destroying animals for sport or decoration. Other rugs were scattered about the gleaming hardwood floor. Occasional chairs, couches, and love seats were placed seemingly at random in the room, lending an atmosphere of casual elegance. End tables and coffee tables were conveniently arranged. In one corner stood a tall, glass-fronted curio cabinet filled with ivory pieces.

After Cody built a fire in the big fireplace, they settled in front of it. He sat on the comfortable couch and Brooke sank down on the bearskin rug. They were relaxed now, almost at ease with each other. And when Cody brought up her abilities, he did so casually, and Brooke responded in the same manner.

"It really shook you when you read my thoughts," he said musingly. "Why? I mean, it's not something new."

"But it is." She frowned a little, gazing into the fire. "It's very rare that I actually read thoughts— clear sentences, I mean. People generally don't think in complete sentences. So what I pick up are images; I know what they're thinking, but I put the thought into words." She turned her head to look at him. "You said you're a troubleshooter in computers?"

"Yes."

"So you've been trained in logic?"

Cody nodded.

"I'll bet you're also exceptionally good at math."

He smiled a little. "That's true. Do my mathematical and logical abilities explain how easily you read my mind?"

"I think so. You're abviously able to focus your thoughts very clearly. In fact"—she lifted a wry brow at him—"you threw them at me."

"Sorry." He didn't look it.

"Sure."

"Really. You have my sincere apologies; I was taught never to throw things."

His solemn tone won a smile from Brooke. "Well. Just don't do it again."

Encouraged, Cody decided that a bit of absurdity would go a long way toward promoting an even more relaxed atmosphere between them. And, being Cody, he dived in headfirst. "It's amazing what a smile will do," he told her confidentially. "I mean, when you walked back into the kitchen last night, I thought, My God, she's as cold as ice!"

Brooke gave him a startled look.

"Well," he explained gravely, "I did say that it wasn't love at *first* sight."

Fighting back a giggle, Brooke managed a brief "Oh."

"But that face!" He went on rapturously, a kind of besotted appreciation running rampant in his voice. "Such perfection! The face that launched a thousand hips—" Cody broke off abruptly, his eyes going wide and ludicrously woeful.

Blinking just once, Brooke murmured politely, "Freudian slip?"

Cody rested his forehead on an upraised hand. "Oh, Lord! Foot-in-mouth disease! Is there no cure?"

"Apparently not."

"I did *not* mean to say that."

"Of course, you didn't."

"My tongue got tangled."

"Happens to the best of us."

"If only thought could wed itself with speech," Cody misquoted mournfully.

"Tennyson," Brooke observed companionably.

Cody stared at her for a moment, then rubbed his hands together like a dastardly villain. "Ah-ha! I see I've found someone to sharpen my poetic sword on. Be warned, woman—poetry is my second language."

She lifted an eyebrow at him. "Really? Well, then, sharpen away."

Noting her slight smile, Cody quoted thoughtfully, " 'Flushed and confident.' "

Still smiling, Brooke murmured, "The flush comes from the nearness of the fire. The confidence comes from lots of reading. And the quotation is from Ibsen."

Cody inclined his head in a small salute and racked his brain. " 'I propose to fight it out on this line, if it takes all winter,' " he said, altering the quotation's last word.

Brooke started laughing. "Not exactly a poet! That was Ulysses S. Grant, and *he* was going to fight all summer."

" 'Understand a plain man in his plain meaning,' " Cody told her in an offended tone.

Soothingly Brooke said, "It's always easy to fall

back on Shakespeare when one runs out of other poets, isn't it?"

Cody visibly gritted his teeth. " 'Victory is not a name strong enough for such a scene.' "

"Lord Nelson."

" 'We are not interested in the possibilities of defeat; they do not exist.' "

"Queen Victoria. You're not a poet's poet, are you? You just like words put together well."

" 'With native humor temp'ring virtuous rage,' " Cody warned awfully.

"Pope."

Cody put his head in his hands. " 'And like a thunderbolt he fails.' "

"Tennyson."

"Uncle!" Cody raised his head and made the traditional "time out" gesture with his hands. "I give up already! I can see I'll have to read up before I cross poetic swords with you again."

"You started it," she reminded him mildly.

A gleam was born in Cody's golden eyes. "How about a game of poker?" he asked with deceptive casualness.

Brooke wasn't deceived. "You wouldn't win," she murmured.

Cody grimaced slightly. "Pepper taught you to cheat?"

"No."

"But?"

Her smile growing, Brooke said, "There's a deck of cards in that end table. Shuffle them and put them facedown on the coffee table, and I'll show you why you wouldn't find it easy to defeat me in a card game."

Cody followed the directions, beginning to guess what would happen.

"The top card," she told him easily, "is a ten of clubs."

He turned the top card faceup. Ten of clubs.

"The six of hearts is next."

It was.

"Jack of diamonds."

Silently Cody turned up the card. Still silent, he turned up ten more cards one at a time. Each card was exactly as she called it. He finally sat back and gazed across at her amused face. "Lord, you'd be worth a fortune to a professional gambler."

Brooke laughed. "Afraid not. Under pressure I miss every time."

"You couldn't have read my mind," Cody noted, "because I didn't see the faces of the cards."

She shrugged. "Like a lot of psychics, I have a lesser second ability; I can predict the turn of the cards."

Hurt . . .

Brooke gasped in spite of herself, her gaze moving toward the back of the lodge. It was there—outside. She could feel its pain and confusion, its fear. There was a sensation—almost a scent—of wildness in the jumbled images, in the pain. And she was afraid to break through her wall and reach out to it.

Because it wasn't human.

She rose to her feet, even her strong awareness of Cody blocked by a jumble of thoughts and the acid taste of fear. The first time had been a week ago. She had awakened from a peaceful sleep with the confusing, frightening sensation of something else's pain battering her. Immediately the wall lowered by sleep had slammed back up, leaving only the faint echoes of . . . presence.

She had never been so confused or so terrified in her life.

What is it? Why did it come only with the night and reach out to her? And why did its cry of pain stir a primitive terror in her?

The wind wailed suddenly, loudly, and her eyes skittered toward a window. Her guard slipped a little.

Hurt . . . hurt . . . hurt . . .

Brooke closed her eyes, shivering. She couldn't shut it out completely anymore. And it wasn't a thought, not a clear, crystalized thought from a human mind; that was what frightened her. It was just an impression, a sensation of hurt, of pain. It made the hairs rise on the nape of her neck and froze the blood in her veins.

There were never any tracks outside. But then, it had snowed every night for the last week, and the wind had created drifts, obscuring any tangible evidence of a visitor that wasn't human.

Hurt . . .

A part of her wanted to help something in pain, but she was afraid. Terrified. It had to be her imagination—had to be! She didn't believe in inhuman things voicing human thoughts. And she had never before felt this wildness, this primitive sensation. There was intelligence in the wildness, and the anger of a cornered beast.

And now it was here in the light of day, and she could see what it was. But she was afraid to see, afraid of what she'd see if she looked.

Hard hands gripped her shoulders, the very touch of him draining away the spell of that inner cry.

"Brooke! Tell me what you're afraid of!"

She looked up into anxious golden eyes almost blindly for a moment; then her own eyes cleared of the mist of fear. "I—nothing. There's nothing."

"Brooke!" Cody's hands tightened on her shoul-

ders. "Dammit, tell me what you're afraid of!"
Patience had gone by the board, Cody realized,
when he'd seen the swift leap of terror in her green
eyes and the rigid control he'd come to dread grip
her face in stillness.

Hurt . . .

She winced, closing her eyes for a brief moment.
"There's . . . something outside," she murmured,
thinking dimly that if this didn't send him in a
mad dash away from a crazy woman, nothing
would. "For about a week now, but only at night
until a moment ago."

"What are you picking up?" Cody asked quietly,
as if it were the most natural and reasonable question in the world.

Brooke looked up at him wonderingly. "Pain . . .
wildness . . . confusion," she said unsteadily.
"Not—not human."

"An animal of some kind?"

She reached to rub her forehead fretfully. "I don't
know. Yes, I suppose. But I've never sensed an animal before, not even Mister. And, whatever it is, it's
intelligent. It's hurt and I want to help it, but"—
she laughed shakily—"it scares the hell out of me!"

Cody glanced briefly toward the front window,
which showed a still-light fall of blowing snow. He
looked back at her, his hands squeezing slightly
and releasing her. "I'll take a look outside," he told
her, turning away.

Momentarily frozen, Brooke swiftly caught up
with him in the hallway leading to the kitchen.
"Cody, no!"

He didn't respond until they were in the kitchen.
Reaching for the thick jacket still draped over the
back of a chair, he said, "Honey, I have to find out
what's out there. For your peace of mind as well as
my own."

Her heart leaping into her throat at the endearment, Brooke had to swallow hard before she could speak. "I'll go with you."

Cody looked at her steadily for a moment. "Have to face the phantom yourself, I see. Is there a gun in the house?"

She nodded.

"Get it."

Brooke came back into the kitchen moments later wearing her thickly quilted and hooded coat, and carrying a loaded .45 automatic. She handed the gun to Cody, watching while he examined it.

"Cleaned and oiled," he noted approvingly. "You?"

"Josh taught me." Brooke pulled the hood up over her hair, then went to the closet off the kitchen and exchanged her loafers for boots. She followed Cody out the back door, and they stood for a moment on the porch, both listening to the howl of the wind and Brooke listening to something else.

"Where?" Cody asked after one look at her face.

Brooke thrust her hands deep into her pockets and nodded jerkily toward a clump of trees about sixty feet from the back of the house and beside the beaten path leading down to the barn. "Over there."

In step they moved out into the snow, feeling little of the wind but hearing it howling in the trees above them. Snow fell faster now, the flakes still large and wet and coming down almost in a solid curtain of whiteness.

"Careful," Cody warned as quietly as possible over the sound of the wind. "If it's hurt, it's dangerous."

But the closer they came to the trees, the less Brooke feared what was waiting for them there.

Partly because Cody was at her side, partly because she was finally facing the fear and facing it in daylight, and partly because the inner voice she listened to now was a quiet one. She stopped suddenly, staring toward the trees.

Cody followed suit. "What is it?"

"It's coming out," she murmured.

He moved another couple of steps toward the trees, straining his eyes to see clearly. Automatically thumbing off the gun's safety catch, he mentally prepared himself to act quickly when—if—the need arose.

They saw the animal a moment later, and Brooke realized instantly why she'd felt the primitive terror, and why she'd sensed an intelligent wildness as well as pain.

Though pitifully thin, the wolf must have weighed close to two hundred pounds. Gray and white fur showed through the layer of snow, and yellow eyes examined the two humans in turn before settling on Brooke. Moving with an uncanny grace, the wolf slowly pulled itself through the snow toward Brooke, dragging an obviously broken and useless front leg.

Instinctively Cody cocked the gun, and the soft click stopped the wolf. Eerie yellow eyes turned toward him and small, pointed ears pricked up as the creature looked at the man. As if he knew. As if he understood. Then the wolf sank silently down in the snow, rolling over almost onto his back and showing them his vulnerable belly. His tail moved weakly.

Cody hesitated for a moment and then eased the hammer back down. Cautiously holding the gun, which was still pointed at the wolf, he glanced at Brooke and then started slowly toward him. "I don't think he'll attack us. No, stay back!" he warned Brooke softly as she began to move toward the wolf. "I'm not sure, dammit!"

"I am. He won't hurt us, Cody."

"Brooke—"

"He won't hurt us."

"Dammit," Cody muttered, still moving toward the wolf and making sure he had a clear shot just in case. He hoped Brooke was right; he didn't want to be forced to kill such a proud and beautiful creature.

They reached the wolf at the same time, both kneeling in the snow. Brooke reached out slowly to touch the fur between the small pointed ears, gazing into yellow eyes that held a curious reassurance. And when the wolf licked her cold hand, the last of Brooke's fear melted away.

Cody thumbed the safety catch of the gun a second time and slid it into his pocket. Cautiously stroking the fur over a still-muscular shoulder, he looked across and met Brooke's eyes. "Even if he wanted to hurt us," he murmured, "I don't think he has the strength."

"How bad is his leg?" Brooke asked.

The wolf was lying on his side now, his head a little raised and resting against Brooke's thigh as the yellow eyes watched Cody's gently probing touch. After a moment Cody said, "A clean break, I think. It'll have to be splinted. I guess there's something to be said for growing up on a ranch; I know how to splint an animal's broken leg."

Frowning, Brooke said, "I think there are some splints in the big first-aid chest, but they're for people. D'you think. . . . ?"

"We can modify them. Go."

"Cody, I can—"

"No, you can't," he interrupted quietly. "Brooke,

I'm not going to leave you alone with him. Not until we have more experience in his temperament."

Brooke wanted to argue, but the rising wind and the wolf shivering with cold beneath her hand decided her. They had to get the animal inside. Gently easing from beneath the animal's head, she quickly rose to her feet and headed for the house.

She was back in ten minutes, immediately warmed to see that Cody's thigh had replaced her own beneath the wolf's head and that he was stroking the animal comfortingly. She changed places with him smoothly and silently, then watched as he went to work.

The wolf stiffened only once, when his leg was gently straightened, but he didn't make a sound or even offer to bite either of them. Cody silently thanked the Fates that it wasn't a compound fracture; there was no break in the flesh that he could find, and the broken bones seemed to set themselves when he straightened the leg. As quickly and gently as possible, he put the splint in place and fastened it securely.

The moment he finished, the wolf struggled awkwardly to his feet, holding the splinted leg out in front of him. He stood there, swaying a bit, and looked toward the lodge as if he could feel the warmth waiting there.

Cody got up and then bent, sliding one arm cautiously around the powerful chest and the other around the hindquarters.

"Your ankle—"

"It'll hold." Keeping as much of the weight as possible on his good ankle, Cody lifted the wolf very cautiously; he knew that most wild creatures panicked when lifted from their feet. But the wolf remained still and quiet. Cody grimaced as his ankle complained of the additional weight, but as he'd hoped, it held.

"Get a blanket or something to put in front of the fire," he told Brooke. "In the kitchen would be best, I think."

Nodding, she headed quickly toward the house.

Moving slowly, Cody followed her.

Four

The big wolf was placed on a thick pile of blankets before the blazing kitchen fire, and two willing pairs of hands went to work drying him with towels. When that had been done, Brooke and Cody consulted briefly before warming a large pan of chicken broth for their canine guest.

Watching as the wolf began slowly but hungrily to drink the broth, Brooke frowned in thought. "I remember Josh saying something once about feeding a sick dog cooked rice mixed with broth and small bits of meat. He said it was the best and most filling meal for them. D'you agree we should feed him just broth today and then start the rice and meat tomorrow?"

"It sounds right to me," Cody replied. He had removed his jacket and eased himself down on one of the chairs. "The broth'll warm him up and take the edge off his hunger; he probably couldn't stand anything more today."

Brooke looked at Cody for a moment, a new frown drawing her brows together; then she left the room. Returning a moment later, she held the small first-aid kit in her hands. She drew the step stool forward and sat down on it. "I want to have a look at your ankle," she told him firmly.

"Brooke—"

"Hey." She looked up at him with a faint smile. "There are certain advantages to being psychic; I know damn well that you strained that ankle by carrying the wolf. So shut up."

Cody sighed softly. "I'm beginning to realize that there are certain *dis*advantages to your being psychic."

"I wondered when you would."

"Nothing I can't live with though," he added hastily.

Brooke smiled but said nothing. Her smile died, however, when she unwrapped the elastic bandage from his ankle; it was swollen again and looked extremely painful. She got up and left the room again, returning with a pillow from one of the couches and what looked like a wraparound hot water bottle. The pillow was placed on the step stool and Cody's ankle raised to rest on it. Then she went outside long enough to fill a medium-size plastic bucket with snow.

She didn't say a word to the puzzled Cody until she'd spread the rubbery device out on the counter and began filling it with snow. Then she merely said, "Cold compress."

Cody, seeking to take her mind off her obvious concern for him, said lightly, "We can't keep on saying 'the wolf' whenever we talk about our new houseguest. What should we name him?"

"You've already named him," Brooke said.

"Have I? What did I name him?"

"Phantom." Brooke carried the snow-filled rubber cuff back and carefully wrapped it around Cody's ankle, then straightened and smiled at him. "You said that I had to go out and meet the phantom myself; can you think of a better name for him?"

Cody smiled a little. "No. No, I can't." He looked toward the hearth; the wolf was watching them silently. "Hello, Phantom."

Phantom pricked up his ears. His tail thumped once.

Strangely unsurprised, Cody noted, "He knows his name."

"Of course." Brooke poured out two cups of coffee, handing one to Cody and taking the other herself as she sat down across the table from him. "I've seen him before, Cody."

"Really?" Cody sipped his coffee. "When?"

"Well . . . several times. In the fall was the last time. But I've seen him at a distance for three or four years. Up on the ridge usually. He runs with a small pack, and he and another wolf—a black one—seem to be the leaders. I'll bet the black one's his mate."

"Wonder how he broke his leg," Cody mused idly.

Brooke shook her head. "I guess we'll never know."

Cody turned his gaze to Brooke. Oddly fanciful, he found himself telling Phantom's story as if he knew it well. "There was no power struggle within the pack; Phantom's too strong for that. And he's too canny to have fallen into a trap set by hunters. He must have fallen or been kicked while they were hunting. With a broken leg he couldn't hunt and he couldn't lead the pack. So his mate had a choice. She could stay with Phantom and hunt alone for both of them, losing leadership of the pack, or else she could leave him where his chances of survival were good, and come back for him when the leg had time to heal."

Taking up the thread of the story, Brooke went on, "She left him here, where there was no scent of hunters. Maybe she even knew that he could reach out to me for help. There was shelter here, and humans who'd left the pack unmolested in the past, so she believed this would be the best place to leave him. What shall we name her?" Brooke demanded suddenly.

Cody thought. "Psyche," he decided firmly.

Brooke's lips twitched. "Goes well with Phantom," she murmured. "And so, Psyche left Phantom here; we'll have to wait and see if she comes back for him."

"D'you think she will?"

"Yes."

"Is Phantom telling you that, or are you guessing?"

"Neither. I know. And Phantom isn't telling me anything. He's just lying there watching us and he's warm."

"I'm glad he's warm. I wish I could say the same for my ankle."

"It'll take the swelling down."

"Actually it feels pretty good."

"Terrific. The last thing I need is to be snowbound with two cripples."

"Kick a man while he's down, why don't you?"

"My favorite sport."

Casually Cody said, "Tell me about your father."

Brooke stiffened for a moment, then sent him a look that was a combination of wry amusement and guardedness. "You don't sound a warning shot, do you? You just fire away."

"I get results that way."

She was silent for a moment. "You're knocking at the walls, Cody," she said finally.

"I know."

"You promised."

"I promised that I wouldn't move too fast and that I wouldn't batter at the walls. I didn't promise not to knock." His warm golden eyes were searching. "First dragon, Brooke. I have to start somewhere."

She shook her head suddenly. "No dragon." Her eyes were fixed unseeingly on Phantom. "Not exactly. I often wonder if my life would've been different if he'd lived longer. But he died when I was six."

"Tell me about him," Cody prompted softly.

"How?" She laughed shortly. "What does a six-year-old notice about someone she loves? That he was tall and strong and used to throw me up on his shoulder? That he had eyes the color of new grass and a voice I could listen to for hours?" Her voice dropped suddenly, became painful and bitter. "That he loved me so much it made my mother hate me?"

Cody saw the first dragon looming between them, not the father but given life by the father. And he wasn't quite sure how to slay a six-year-old's memory of the tangle of love and hate. He reached across the table to cover her hand, but Brooke snatched it away.

"Don't." Green eyes, filled with misery and confusion and pain, stared into his. "I—I can't think when you touch me. I can't tell you. And you have to know, don't you? You *have* to."

"I have to," he agreed quietly.

Brooke nodded jerkily, falling silent for a while. When Cody was beginning to think she meant to confide nothing more, she finally spoke. "I guess I was about five when I realized Mother didn't like me. She was never demonstrative; Daddy was. But it wasn't that. I was psychic then; I picked up feelings rather than thoughts, and I didn't understand. I always felt . . . twisted and ugly whenever Mother came near me. And she said things out loud to me when Daddy wasn't around. That I was stupid. That I was ugly."

Cody, swallowing anger, began to build a composite picture in his mind of a mother so driven by jealousy of her child that she cruelly undermined her confidence. Because Cody knew instinctively that Brooke had been a beautiful child, an innately sweet and giving child.

So lost in memory that she was unaware of Cody's building anger, Brooke unconsciously validated his thoughts. "I tried to—to win her love. I tried to be a good girl. But no matter what I did, I couldn't win her approval. And I was afraid to tell Daddy what I felt when I was around Mother; I was afraid he'd stop loving me.

"Then Daddy died." Brooke blinked quickly for a moment, adding with unconscious starkness, "I missed him."

Cody had forgotten the throbbing of his ankle, had forgotten the wolf lying quietly on his blankets watching them. He was staring at Brooke's profile and hearing the puzzled anguish of a little girl.

She sighed raggedly. "There wasn't any money, and Mother wasn't trained for anything. She complained bitterly about having to wait on tables or clerk in stores. She ignored me, except when she wanted someone to yell at."

The pain in her voice hurting him more than he

would have believed possible, Cody tried to divert her mind. "Your uncle? Couldn't your mother have turned to him for help?"

Brooke shook her head. "Daddy and Josh had a terrible argument when he married her. Josh thought that Daddy was too young, and that Mother wasn't the wife he needed. They never saw each other again, and Daddy never told Josh about me. Mother—Mother had never met Josh, and she didn't know where he lived. We were living in Alabama then."

"I see."

Brooke picked up her cup and drained the last of the cold coffee, seemingly unaware or uncaring that it was cold. "We lived in a tiny apartment, near enough to a school so that I could walk. And it was when I was in the first grade that everyone began to realize I was . . . different. My teacher noticed it first; I was answering questions before she asked them out loud, and she realized I was probably psychic. She'd graduated from Duke University in North Carolina, and she knew about the work they were doing there in ESP.

"She gave me a few simple tests herself, making them seem like games. Then she arranged a meeting with Mother after school one day. And she told her about my . . . gifts."

Cody watched the still, silent profile for a few moments. He wondered what Brooke was thinking, wondered what had given birth to the diamond hardness he saw now in her face. Then the spell shattered.

Brooke stirred slightly and turned her head to meet his quiet gaze. "That's Chapter One," she said lightly. "Let's leave Chapter Two for later, shall we?"

The forced lightness didn't deceive Cody; he

heard the strain in her voice and saw it in her eyes. And memories, he'd discovered, were best pulled from the dark recesses a few at a time; yanking open the door and allowing them all to rush in at once was possible only if one's memories were mostly happy ones.

"Fine," he agreed softly.

Restlessly she murmured, "You haven't said much."

"Just trying to decide whether to use my magic sword or my thrice-blessed dagger on those dragons," he said solemnly.

In spite of herself Brooke started to smile. Wonderingly she realized that the recounting of her painful memories hadn't hurt nearly as much as she'd believed they would. And Cody, the warm glow in his eyes undiminished, seemed so understanding! Of course, the worst was yet to come, but Brooke realized that Chapter Two, and all those chapters to follow, would come more easily.

She was grateful for that. Grateful to Cody and to his persistence. But she was also nervous and uneasy; she would be stripping layer after layer of her protective wall away until only her bare and wounded self remained. Would those half-healed wounds reopen when exposed to the light?

Would Cody hurt her?

Brooke pushed the silent questions away, and sought to follow his lead in lightening the atmosphere between them. "Thrice-blessed? I thought that *twice* did the trick."

"Not with your dragons," Cody responded feelingly. "S'matter of fact, I may have to get the thing blessed again. However, since three's a magic number, we'll hope it does the trick."

"Three's a magic number?"

"You should know."

"I'm psychic, Cody—not a witch."

"My mistake."

"See that it doesn't happen again."

"Or?"

"Or I'll feed you soup made of bats' wings and eye of newt, and you'll turn into a frog."

"But then you could kiss me, and I'd turn back into a prince."

"*Back* into a prince?"

"I'd hoped you wouldn't notice that."

"I notice everything."

"Uh, I think I'll practice reading your mind," Cody announced calmly.

"Why?"

"Because this one-sided business is very unfair."

"What brought this up?"

"I was just thinking."

"Oh. Okay, then—practice. What am I thinking right now?"

"You're hungry."

Brooke stared at him, startled. "That's—right."

Cody smiled modestly, then started chuckling. "I'd better confess before you dip into my mind and discover that I didn't dip into yours."

After mentally untangling his sentence, Brooke shot him a suspicious glare. "You didn't read my mind?"

"Nope."

"Then how did you know . . . ?"

"Well, I'm pretty observant myself, you know. Just before you challenged me to read your mind, you looked toward the refrigerator. So I guessed."

"Princes don't resort to sneaky tactics," Brooke reproved him sternly.

"They do if princesses have ESP."

"Even if. It's unprincely."

"All's fair."

"Don't start throwing clichés at me."

"I've already told you that I don't throw things."

"You're looking more and more like a frog, pal."

"Trust me, lady. I'm a prince."

That plea was made with such a soulful look that Brooke had to bite back a laugh. Shaking her head, she rose from her chair. "And on that note I'm going to fix lunch. Any preferences?"

"I have a sudden aversion to frogs' legs."

"Funny."

Cody looked mildly pleased with himself. "Apropos, I thought."

Brooke sighed. "Right. I repeat. Any preferences?"

"Nope. Nary a one."

"Then I'll see what's in the cupboard."

"Do that, Mother Hubbard."

"I knew you wouldn't be able to resist that."

"If I'm getting predictable, I'll quit," Cody said, injured.

"Not predictable." Brooke reflected. "Just not surprising."

Cody frowned. "I'll have to do something about that."

Rummaging in the cabinets and refrigerator for the makings of lunch, Brooke sent him an amused look, but said nothing. Surprise, she knew, was the essence of many a battle plan, and she wondered if Cody had chosen deliberately to keep her slightly off-balance. Why? The better to fight her dragons?

Something clenched inside of her suddenly as Brooke remembered what she'd very nearly forgotten: that this man claimed to be in love with her. She found herself staring blankly at a box she'd taken from a cabinet and wondering rather desperately why she kept forgetting it. Was it a part of

Cody's plan, or was her own mind playing tricks on her?

"Why're you staring at a box of breakfast cereal as if it were whispering the secrets of a universe?" Cody asked politely.

She blinked at him. "Oh . . . just thinking."

Cody's eyes narrowed suddenly, and then one corner of his mouth lifted in a funny little grin. "Hey, I think I'm beginning to get the hang of it. You were thinking about me, weren't you?"

"That's called vanity," Brooke managed firmly.

He looked hurt. "You weren't thinking of me?"

Brooke shoved the box of cereal back into the cabinet, more rattled than she looked—she hoped. Ignoring his question, she asked, "Is beef stew all right with you? We can give the leftovers to Phantom tomorrow."

"Fine."

He was watching her, Brooke knew. And with a disquieting smile, dammit. He hadn't read her mind. No way. He'd just guessed again. She'd have enough trouble coping with a dragonslaying prince without adding ESP to all his other virtues.

Virtues?

Damn the man.

After lunch Brooke removed the cold compress from Cody's ankle to find that the swelling had begun to go down again. She bound it up in an elastic bandage, then found a pair of crutches left over from Josh's broken leg, and told Cody that if he put any weight on the ankle before she said he could, she'd throw him out into the snow to fend for himself. Somewhat meekly Cody promised to obey the command.

The promised storm was fully blown by three

o'clock, the wind howling outside, and a mixture of snow and sleet pelting the windowpanes. Brooke had turned on the kitchen radio, and the weather forecast from Butte was not in the least encouraging—unless one were a polar bear. Up to two feet of snow was forecast, and the announcer cheerfully mentioned power failures and impassable roads. He also told listeners to have a nice day.

Tacitly agreeing not to leave their canine houseguest alone in the kitchen, Cody and Brooke settled down at the kitchen table with a Scrabble game. Phantom, further warmed and filled by a second helping of chicken broth, blinked sleepily and then seemed to doze off, his pointed ears twitching occasionally at the sounds of their voices.

"That's not a word."

"It is, too. Asphodel. It's a Mediterranean plant."

Cody looked suspicious. "Are you a botanist?"

"No. It was a hobby of Josh's."

"Great."

"I guess I should tell you that Josh tutored me for years. And he was a brilliant man."

"Uh-huh." Cody sighed.

"Buck up. If you can just make a word with that Z, you'll beat me. More points, you know."

Cody frowned in thought for a moment, and then triumphantly produced ZENITH.

Brooke wrestled silently with an X for a while before coming up with XENON. She smiled at Cody across the table. "We've conquered two of the roughest letters; it should be downhill from now on."

"Oh, yeah? What can I spell with this Q?"

"I can think of six words right off the top of my head."

Cody stared at her, then defiantly spelled out QUACK on the board.

"You mind's telling on you," Brooke observed.

"I beg your pardon?"

"Quack. As in charlatan. You're doubting me."

"For your information I was thinking of the sound a duck makes."

She bit back a laugh. "My mistake."

"That quite all right."

"You're very gracious," she said approvingly.

"I'm a hell of a guy."

"And modest."

That first day spent together told Cody quite a lot. Though beginning to piece together the events of her past through the little Brooke had told him so far, he discovered that he was actually learning more about her just by being with her in the present. With the wolf comfortably inside with them now, she was no longer haunted by a mental cry she didn't understand and was far more relaxed than Cody had yet seen her.

And throughout the afternoon his seemingly casual but intent observation of her behavior gave him clues as to how to go about slaying the dragons standing between them.

He noticed first of all that Brooke was intensely wary of being touched; drawing away seemed almost a reflex with her. While she could touch him with apparent calm when dealing with his injured ankle, or allow him to lean on her as she had the night before, the most casual of *unnecessary* physical contact caused an inner stiffening that Cody could sense more than feel.

With the neatly logical mind that made him a wizard with computers, Cody sifted the possibilities until he arrived at one that seemed to explain Brooke's wariness. Gradually he realized that the inner stiffening he felt was simply a shoring up of her mental wall. Physical contact, he decided, probably made her more vulnerable to mental contact.

That explanation satisfied Cody's critical scrutiny, so he set his mind to finding a way of dealing with the problem. The answer promised a great many sleepless nights for him; to become accustomed to anything a person had to be gradually exposed to it. And while his own inner conviction and strong desires might have led him to push Brooke into a relationship she wasn't ready for, his innate wisdom and a caution born of love joined together in the voice of reason.

So Cody held on to his willpower with every atom of control and set about getting Brooke accustomed to being touched undemandingly. He had to overcome instincts within her, instincts that had been sharpened by her need to guard her mind. He slowly and carefully had to invade the private territory that every human being claimed and marked as personal; had to convince Brooke that there was no threat to herself in allowing him so close.

Brooke tensed slightly when Cody reached over to take her hand in a gentle clasp. They were sitting on a couch before a blazing fire in the sunken den. Supper was over and the wind was howling in the darkness outside.

His hand was large and warm, its strength only a promise since there was no force in his grip. Brooke, her unusual senses reacting to the contact as iron to a magnet, instantly and expertly slammed the door opening between them. She felt the lightness that had been the rule since lunch evaporate, felt tension and uneasiness creep into her awareness. She wanted to pull her hand away, but couldn't seem to, and she couldn't say a word.

Luckily for both Cody's plans and Brooke's composure, Phantom came into the room just then to create a timely diversion. The wolf moved steadily, swinging his splinted leg with a touch of awkwardness but seemingly in no pain. He negotiated the step down into the room cautiously, then came toward the pair watching him from the couch. He sniffed at the bearskin rug before the hearth and then, concluding that it wasn't actively hostile, sank down on the snowy whiteness with an almost human sigh.

"I guess he didn't want to be alone," Cody noted.

"Looks that way." Brooke tried to forget the hands clasped on the cushion between them, but her awareness of Cody—having nothing to do with her ESP, she realized—wouldn't let her forget. "Uh . . . how's the ankle?" she asked rather hastily.

Cody glanced at his bound ankle, which was resting on a pillow on top of the coffee table. "Fine." He sent a faint grimace toward the crutches resting against a nearby chair. "You'll be able to put those things back in the closet soon."

"When the ankle's healed and not a minute sooner," she told him firmly.

"Yes, Doctor," he murmured with a smile.

"Don't mock me."

He lifted her hand and kissed it briefly. "Wouldn't think of it."

Brooke stared fiercely at the fire. Lips, she reassured herself silently, were very human things. They didn't cause electric shocks; therefore, she hadn't felt an electric shock when Cody's lips had touched her hand. Period. It was all her imagination. She shifted restlessly. "Cody—"

"The wind's dying down, don't you think?" He cut her off with ruthless intent.

"No. No, it acts like that up here sometimes. Like the eye of a hurricane, or something. It'll probably pick back up in a few minutes." She hesitated. "Cody—"

"D'you think this storm will turn into an actual blizzard?" he asked casually, cutting her off yet again. "I've never been through a blizzard before."

Brooke gave him a frustrated look, making one weak and fruitless attempt to pull her hand from his grasp. "You don't go *through* a blizzard unless you're out in it; if you're lucky enough to be indoors, you just wait it out. And, yes, it sounds like a blizzard to me."

"Good," Cody said with every evidence of satisfaction.

"Good? Cody—"

"I've always wanted to be snowbound."

"*Will* you let me finish a sentence?" she demanded irritably.

"Sorry." Golden eyes that were fathoms deep and impossibly limpid gazed into hers. "You were saying?"

With a tremendous effort Brooke tore her gaze away and stared into the fire. Why did she suddenly feel that she'd been pulled into those golden pools and sucked under? "I forgot," she murmured. Truthfully. What had she been about to say? Protest. That was it. She'd been about to protest his hand-holding business. But it didn't seem important now.

Feeling mildly pleased by his victory in the small and silent skirmish, Cody surged ahead in an effort to hold on to his lead. "Are we completely cut off from civilization, barring the radio and the Sno-Cat?" he asked interestedly.

Absently Brooke said, "Until they repair the phone line. Since you fixed the generator, we can do without electricity from town. And we have enough provisions to last the winter; I always stock in the fall."

"How long d'you think the storm will last?"

"Could be days." Her own words prompted misgivings, but Brooke ignored them; worrying wouldn't change anything. "Storm systems can be tricky up here in the mountains. It's almost as if they turn in on themselves and grow more powerful instead of weaker."

Cody looked at her for a long moment, suddenly realizing something. "There are no guests coming next week, are there?" he asked gently.

Brooke wasn't surprised; she shook her head slightly. "No. Because of the weather, I rarely take guests this time of year. I just told you that hoping you'd leave."

"And now?"

"And now what?" She refused to look at him.

"Are you glad I stayed?"

Lightly she asked, "Fishing?"

"Fishing."

Brooke was afraid to meet his clear golden eyes, afraid that his gaze would pull the truth out of her. His very presence was tugging at her now, demanding truth. Demanding honesty. And she wanted to scream at him suddenly for demanding anything of her.

"Never mind, Brooke." Intuitively Cody sensed her abrupt resistance, the flare of emotions. He silently cursed himself for pushing; they had a long way to go yet. He squeezed her hand lightly and then released it. "It's been a—long and eventful day. Why don't we turn in?"

Silent, she rose to her feet, reaching for the crutches and handing them to him. Her hand felt strangely alone without the warmth of his, cold and alone. But she didn't want to think of that. She concentrated on the wail of the wind and on the wolf lying on the bearskin rug.

"He'll be alone again," she murmured.

On his feet and braced by the crutches, Cody looked down at Phantom. "He'll be all right. He knows where his water is, and he knows we're in the house with him. He'll be fine, Brooke."

She nodded, preceding Cody from the room. He left her at her door with a quiet good night, going on down the hall to his own room. Brooke closed the door and leaned back against it for a moment, then automatically began getting ready for bed.

Preparing to slide between the sheets, Brooke paused for a moment and looked toward her door. She went over and opened it, discovering Phantom standing out in the hall. He looked up at her, his tail waving once. Brooke glanced down the hall toward Cody's bedroom, then stepped back to admit the wolf.

"Come on in," she invited softly. "We just won't tell Cody."

Moments later, lulled by the steady wail of the wind outside and by the quiet presence of Phantom on the rug by her bed, Brooke slipped into a deep and dreamless sleep.

Five

A week passed, and then another. That first blizzard lasted three days and, with Nature apparently in one of her infrequent fits of regularity, was followed by overnight storms every three days for those two weeks. Cody's repair job on the generator held; they had plenty of power and food. Insisting that Cody remain inside and not risk the treacherous footing outdoors, Brooke made the daily trips to feed Mister and bring in wood.

Experience of Montana winters had bred self-sufficiency and strength in Brooke; she coped easily with the outside chores and accepted the violence of the weather with tolerance.

They quickly discovered that Phantom was a thoughtful and considerate houseguest; after the first couple of days of needed rest, he politely requested to go outside once or twice a day, going to one or the other of his human companions and nudging gently before heading pointedly for the back door. The wolf was more adept at swinging his splinted leg now, and seemed to have no trouble coping with the uneven drifts of snow outside. While one of his companions waited at the open door, Phantom would disappear around the corner of the house. He would return within moments, then stand patiently inside the kitchen while his thick coat was brushed free of clinging snow.

He was a silent creature, never whining or yelping as a domesticated dog would have done. Only a faint rumbling growl would emerge from his throat when, after a meal, he'd settle down before the fire in the den with his humans for company.

Brooke and Cody, both instinctively companionable with animals, spoke casually to the wolf as if he were a third person. And every night, after Cody's bedroom door had closed, Phantom would make his way silently to Brooke's door and await admittance. Brooke always left the door slightly open, and Phantom was always back in the den or kitchen whenever Cody got up in the morning.

As for Brooke and Cody, the enforced intimacy of being virtually snowbound together with only a silent wolf and each other for company would have either drawn them closer together or else set them inexorably apart.

It drew them together.

Resolutely patient and undemanding, Cody set about teaching Brooke to trust him. They played chess, checkers and Chinese checkers, and Monopoly. They carried on ridiculous conversations in which quotations substituted for dialogue and became progressively more obscure and absurd. Both shared a passion for mysteries, and together they would construct plots and spend hours discussing possible solutions. They talked about everything two different people would find interesting.

They didn't talk about Brooke's dragons.

More than once during those days, Brooke would have continued her story if Cody had asked her to. He didn't. Cody was waiting for a sign. A physical sign.

He had continued to touch Brooke casually and undemandingly. He held her hand, touched her cheek lightly, tugged playfully at the ponytail she occasionally wore. He slipped an arm around her shoulders whenever they sat side by side, hugged her with first one arm and then gradually both. And always, Cody waited for the stiffening that warned him to withdraw from Brooke's private space.

Cody always respected her instinctive reaction. That respect and his patience began to pay off during the second week; Brooke gradually came to accept his touch without stiffening at all. She accepted as casually as he gave, becoming more and more relaxed in his company.

But still Cody waited. Knowing without being told that Brooke had known few demonstrative people in her life, he realized that when she finally reached out for someone—if even with an automatic, casual touch—it would be the first step in learning how to open up to another person. And Cody wanted to be that other person.

The breakthrough, when it came, went unnoticed by Brooke. But Cody was so jubilant that he only just stopped himself from laughing out loud.

"I washed the dishes," Cody reported cheerfully as Brooke came into the den after making her midafternoon trip down to the barn to feed Mister.

"You did that for me?" Brooke patted him lightly on the head as she came around the couch to kneel in front of the coffee table. "How sweet." She frowned thoughtfully down at the Monopoly game her trip to the barn had interrupted.

Just a little thing—a pat on the head. But it was the first time Brooke had touched him casually and absentmindedly and, to Cody, it was the reward for many restless nights. "Your move," he managed to remind her easily.

"I've got a feeling," she said darkly, "that I'll end up in jail." Cautiously she rolled the dice.

And had to go directly to Jail.

Cody lifted an eyebrow at her. "Precognition?"

Brooke sighed. "No. Just experience with sheer bad luck."

Cody made a "tut-tut" sound. "Your luck'll turn. *I've* got a feeling."

"Precognition?" she asked dryly.

"Horse sense."

"Ah. I thought only horses had that."

"Sheathe your claws, you little cat."

"Was I clawing? I beg your pardon, I'm sure."

"You've been clawing from the start," Cody pointed out, wounded. "The moment we met, you knocked me flat on my—"

"Language!"

". . . ego." Cody lifted the other brow at her. "And you've been sticking pins in my ego ever since."

"I never!"

"Oh, yes. In fact, you see before you a quivering mass of insecurity. A bundle of nerves. A man bordering on severe trauma."

Brooke blinked at him. "Goodness. Did I do all that?"

"Yes."

"Sorry."

"*Sorry*, she says! The woman totally destroys a man, and she says she's sorry. As if that'll help! Right, Phantom?" The wolf, lying on the bearskin rug near Brooke, thumped his tail once and watched them out of sleepy yellow eyes.

Reasonably Brooke said, "Well, I don't know what else I could say. How, by the way, did I commit this act of destruction?"

Forced to the point, Cody neatly evaded it. "You've broken my spirit!" he accused mournfully.

"How?" she repeated.

"Here I am," he said sadly, "prepared to do battle in the best dragonslaying tradition, and the fair lady won't even allow me to defend her!"

Since this kind of playful tiptoeing-around-the-subject had been going on for nearly a week, Brooke was accustomed to it. "I'll let you get me out of Jail," she offered helpfully.

"Poor substitute," Cody sniffed with disdain.

"C'mon, be princely. Get me out of Jail."

"Maybe I'd better leave you there; you can't run away from me now."

"I couldn't run far anyway. The weather, you know."

"This is true." Cody reflected for a moment. "All right, then. I'll trade you the get-out-of-Jail card."

"Trade it for what?"

"Chapter Two," he said lightly.

Absently toying with the dice, Brooke looked up suddenly. She saw the golden eyes resting on her in gentle inquiry, felt no demand from Cody. Only a quiet question. With exaggerated care she placed the dice on the gameboard and clasped her hands together on her thighs. "It's time, huh?" she murmured.

"I think so. But I won't push if you're not ready."

She gazed at him steadily for a moment, her

green eyes naked in their uncertainty. Then she squared her shoulders. "All right."

Cody leaned back on the couch, deliberately withdrawing from even the most tenuous contact with her. She would reach for him this time, he thought. He hoped. He needed her to reach for him. Needed her to need him. "What happened after your mother discovered your were psychic?" he asked.

Brooke took a deep breath. "My teacher told her about the research being done at some of the universities and about the parapsychological institutes. And I suppose she meant to be helpful when she told Mother that some of the institutes paid . . . subjects . . . to be studied. Mother contacted some of the places, and the next thing I knew, we were on a plane.

"That was the beginning. Most of the researchers were kind to me, and they made it all seem like a game." Her voice dropping to the gruff, detached tone Cody remembered from their first meeting, Brooke recalled the "games."

"I'm thinking of a toy, Brooke, what is it? There's a man in the next room, Brooke; what picture is he drawing? I'm going to ask you a question, Brooke, in my head; I want you to answer it out loud. I'm thinking, Brooke; what am I thinking? These cards all gave pictures, Brooke; I want you to tell me what the picture on each card is before I turn it over."

Brooke closed her eyes for a moment, then went on. "I was . . . studied off and on for years. And when the reputable institutes and universities had learned all they could from me, Mother found some that were less reputable. That's when the publicity began. Pictures and interviews and poor, foolish people—believing that I could look into their minds and somehow straighten out their troubled lives. People who were afraid of me and yet wanted to . . . touch me. Staring. Always staring at me."

Rising suddenly to her feet, Brooke began to move restlessly around the room. Touching an object here and there, not looking at Cody. Still speaking in that gruff, detached voice.

"And then Mother met a self-styled promoter. He handled mostly carnivals and sideshows. When he looked at me, he saw a gold mine. To this day I think he believed that I was just a ten-year-old kid with a gift for tricking people. He didn't believe in anything he couldn't spend or put into the bank, but he knew how to attract people to a show. And he built a show around me."

His pent-up anger needing release, Cody muttered, "How could your mother allow—"

Brooke laughed painfully. "Allow? She loved every minute of it. We went from small town to small town just like a circus. I was billed as a mentalist and stood up on stage reading minds. The promoter and Mother were making money; they were happy. The crowds that came to the show were always a mixed lot. There was always a heckler or two in the audience who called me a phony, and some called me a witch or worse. My . . . gift was hailed as being from God and cursed as being from the devil. Oh, I heard it all."

"But the authorities. School," Cody said, trying to find something acceptable, something normal in her life.

Staring into the case containing the ivory pieces her uncle had collected, Brooke shrugged. "Occasionally a concerned citizen would get suspicious and call the police. But the promoter was canny and Mother always had good instincts; we usually stayed one jump ahead of the truant officer. There was always another little town over the horizon. Another audience."

Whirling suddenly, Brooke came to stand at the end of the couch, staring down at Cody with bitter, painful memories in her green eyes. "Can you imagine what it was like? Standing up in front of all those people in that ridiculous long black robe . . . voices battering at me as if I were in the middle of a wild crowd—but they were *inside my head.* I couldn't get away from them, I couldn't shut them out. My head hurt all the time, and sometimes I felt as if I'd explode. The people were afraid of me, and I didn't know why. They were afraid of me, and sometimes they hated me because they didn't understand . . . and I didn't understand either."

Her eyes burned with unshed tears and memories. "They were afraid of me, but they were also hungry—always demanding, always wanting more. And I couldn't shut them out!"

So still that he might have been formed of stone, Cody looked up at her and forced himself to wait.

Barely seeing him through the hazy wash of tears, Brooke was consciously aware for the first time of a hunger of her own. A need. A need for the human contact she'd denied herself for years. Memories of those faceless, demanding eyes rose up before her, causing something deep inside her to shy away from thoughts of contact. But then, as she blinked back the tears and the memories, she saw Cody's familiar eyes gazing steadily at her. Golden eyes full of compassion and understanding, and a muted anger for her and for what she'd gone through as a child. Without thought her hand reached out jerkily toward him, like the hand of a puppet, its strings sharply tugged.

The almost helpless gesture won an immediate response from Cody. He caught her hand in his own, drawing her down gently until she was sitting close beside him. He slipped one arm around her shoulders comfortingly, still holding her hand warmly. And in his fierce determination to keep his own physical desires at bay, Cody found that he himself was more open, more receptive to another's feelings that he'd ever been before. His intuition had picked up the signals Brooke had unconsciously sent, revealing her dragons to him, stripped of their mystique and of half their power.

"You're punishing yourself, honey," he said softly.

She looked at him, uneasy, aware on some level of her mind that Cody had somehow learned something about her that she didn't know consciously herself. "I—I don't know what you mean," she murmured, grateful for the warmth of his nearness and yet fearful that it was the first step toward the demands that had driven her to hide inside herself.

Cody hesitated for a split second, knowing that what he was about to say would cut, and cut deeply. But he realized that this wound, at least, had to be reopened to allow the poison of bitterness to escape. He only wished that he wasn't the one forced to use the knife. Not when she'd only just learned to trust him.

Carefully he said, "You talked about the audience always being hungry, always demanding, and I'm sure that's true. But it was your mother who demanded the most, wasn't it, Brooke? She was the one who demanded that you step out on a stage and . . . perform."

Restlessly Brooke tried to draw away from him, finding that he wouldn't let her go this time. "We had no money," she murmured tightly. "My mother had to find some way of supporting us."

"Stop defending her!" Cody ordered flatly. "She exploited you. She exploited you and you hate her for that."

"It isn't natural to hate your mother," Brooke whispered, staring straight in front of her and sitting stiffly at Cody's side.

"That's why you're punishing yourself," he said quietly. When she turned her head almost reluctantly to look at him, Cody added, "You think it isn't natural, that children are supposed to love their parents unreservedly. You felt her hate when you were too young to understand it, but you kept fighting it. You kept trying to win her approval. And when she demanded that you step out onto a stage and open your mind to the worst and most degrading kind of abuse, you did it. Because you didn't want her to hate you. By doing that, you ended up hating her."

Brooke opened her mouth to speak, but Cody rushed ahead. "You were an abused child, honey. And a victim of guilt—your own. You tried so hard to win your mother's love that it nearly destroyed you. And when you finally broke away from her domination, you punished yourself for your hatred of her by locking yourself away—mentally in your own mind, and physically way out here in the back of beyond."

"I had to have privacy," Brooke managed to object, hearing the quiver in her voice.

"That wasn't the only reason, Brooke."

"It was!"

"No. You hate your mother. *Admit it!* Dammit, Brooke, face that dragon and then put it behind you! You're hurting yourself, punishing yourself needlessly; face the fact that she deserved your hate and then, dammit, forget it!"

Instinctively, silently, Brooke tried to deny the

truth of his words, but his clear, concise perception defeated her. Memories she'd kept locked away flooded her mind with cruel images. Her mother pushing her out onto the stage that first time, exposing her to the countless thoughts of strangers. Her mother coldly commenting to the promoter that her daughter's only talent should be put to good use. Shrill cruelty in a voice thick with alcohol. The calculation in her mother's eyes as her thin, childish body had begun to bloom into womanhood. The hateful words. Always the hateful words . . .

"Brooke . . ."

His voice. Lancing through the blackened curtain of memories as if it were truly a magic sword. Filled with regret and pain and an understanding such as she had never known. Deep and soft and rough, like the gold nugget Josh had once shown her. It drew her like a magnet, filled her with a sort of feverish wonder. Gold fever, she thought hazily. And there was no cure for gold fever.

Tears spilled from her eyes at last, tears that washed the bitterness clean and cooled the hate. She felt the warmth of his arms holding her close, heard the soothing murmur of his wonderful voice. And she cried, finally, for the mother she had blindly loved . . . and just as blindly hated.

Years of bitterness and confused pain couldn't be erased in moments, but Brooke made a start then. And if there was fear in her rough, jerky sobs, Cody didn't realize it. But Brooke did. Somewhere in the deepest part of her consciousness, she realized dimly that she was facing up to more than the dragons of her past. She was facing the dragons of her future as well. And that frightened her.

He didn't breathe fire. He didn't lift a primeval

head high above the waves in an omen of doom. He didn't threaten destruction or terror. Instead, he made her laugh and cry and reach for a part of herself she was afraid to touch. He drew her to him with golden eyes and a golden voice, and made her feel that she was a normal woman. And he was the very dragon he'd described himself: an area of unexplored, possibly terrifying darkness. The uncharted seas that Brooke was afraid to set sail for.

Cody held her and lèt her cry, unaware that from the ashes of an old conflict a new one had risen. He knew only that the largest dragon standing between them was now merely a shadow without substance. It was a beginning, and it was all he had asked for.

When the sobs finally tapered off to muffled hiccups, Cody reached for a handkerchief and gently raised her chin. He wiped her eyes, then held the scrap of cloth for her and ordered softly, "Blow."

Meekly Brooke obeyed the order, long wet lashes hiding her eyes from his too perceptive gaze. She wasn't a shy woman; she'd faced too many crowds—hostile and otherwise—to be shy. But at that moment she hardly knew where to look or what to say. She only knew that the confusion within her was even greater than it had been before the tears.

"You should hang out a shingle," she murmured at last. "You make a pretty fair armchair psychologist."

Following her lead and his own instincts, Cody kept it light. "That's me—Doctor Nash. You'll please note that my couch is comfortable.

"Oh, very."

Solemnly Cody said, "But we've got to stop meeting like this; people will begin to talk."

Brooke finally met the warm golden eyes, discovering that they were still warm and now contained a light of mischief. To her surprise she found that she could respond easily to his humor, and wondered vaguely if the man was a warlock. "What people?" she asked reasonably. "There's only us."

"People always know," Cody told her darkly.

"Ah." Not at all surprised, Brooke watched her hand reach up to smooth back the lock of thick golden hair that had fallen over his forehead. And still not surprised, she realized that she'd wanted to do that for days now. His face was so expressionless, she thought dimly. So still and expressionless.

Cody kept a finger-and-toehold on his willpower. His gentlemanly instincts told him that this was hardly the moment to unleash the fierce desire he felt for her—but the instincts were very nearly overridden. He kissed her lightly on the nose, and it was like a starving man being chained down in front of a banquet.

Only a scent of promise.

An instinct of her own told Brooke that she was teetering right on the edge of a dark pit, and she shied away. Feeling a nudge from the wolf, she used that as an excuse to gently disentangle herself and rise to her feet. "I think Phantom wants out," she murmured.

"Don't get lost," Cody ordered lightly. But when Brooke and the wolf had gone, he rose from the couch and began wandering around the room. The crutches had been abandoned; his walk was even and firm. He moved restlessly, not quite aimlessly, as though looking for something he couldn't find.

They never got back to the Monopoly game.

*　　*　　*

It was perhaps nature's apology for her ESP, but Brooke never remembered her dreams. She'd always slept in peace and silence, what dreams she dreamed never disturbing her. Until that night. . . .

The little boat was sailing merrily across a glass-smooth sea, its sails billowing and snapping in the brisk wind. Brooke turned her face to the salt spray, feeling alive and wonderful. Then she let herself doze in the sun. When she awoke, it was to find the sky a leaden gray and the wind wailing in sails shredded by its force.

Panicked, Brooke could see land nowhere in sight, and her boat was plowing through waves growing higher by the moment. She couldn't control the boat; it was being tossed by an angry sea toward an unexplored horizon. She clung to the mast, watching in horrified fascination as the little boat was drawn into the outer circle of a tremendous whirlpool. The boat circled lazily at first, seemingly barely moving. But then it increased its speed until it was spinning sickeningly. Brooke felt herself scream, but no sound could be heard above the awful roaring of the monster whirlpool. . . .

Everything went black and still. The boat had stopped, its keel hung on something. As light gradually penetrated, Brooke could see that the boat was hanging on the edge of a pit, and the pit was the blackest black she'd ever seen or imagined. Terrified to move, knowing that only a step could send the boat out of balance and push it over the edge, she held on to the mast.

And then, out of the pit came a curious sound: whistling. Cheerful, lively, the sound was so incongruous as to be fascinating. And as she watched, a dragon reared its head from the pit.

It was a multicolored dragon, feathered rather than scaled. The feathers were mostly gold. It had golden eyes and a face that was oddly undragon-like; it reminded her of something, but she didn't know what. It had long claws on its dragon feet, which it proceeded absently to buff against its chest-feathers as it hovered there in midair and looked at her.

"Hello."

Brooke told herself that this was a dream. Definitely a dream, and she couldn't seem to wake herself up. There was really no boat, no pit, and definitely no dragon. But the mast beneath her clutching fingers felt like real wood. . . .

"Hello," she said, deciding to make the most of this.

"You're late," the dragon accused sternly.

She blinked at it. "Am I?"

"Certainly. I expected you days ago." The dragon inspected its neatly buffed claws and then lifted a feathered eyebrow at her.

Brooke rather cautiously let go of the mast and moved toward the bow of the boat. "It won't go over, will it?" she asked fearfully.

"Of course not," the dragon scoffed. "You'll have to jump."

She halted a couple of feet back from the pointed bow. "I will not," she told the dragon decidedly. "Then I'd be in the pit. And dragons eat people."

An absurdly hurt expression twisted the dragon's face. "I wouldn't do that. Besides, I need you."

"For an appetizer?"

"Oh, no. Certainly not." The dragon floated a bit nearer, its big golden eyes peering at her serenely. In a confidential tone it said, "You see, I'm actually a prince."

Brooke crossed her arms over her breasts. "Of course, you are," she agreed politely.

"Really," the dragon insisted, clearly sensing doubt.

She stared at him. "Look, this is my dream. Now, I'd be willing to accept a frog-prince in my dream, but not a dragon-prince. It just isn't done."

The dragon scratched what might have been an ear with one long claw. He seemed perturbed. Doubtfully he said, "Well, I know it's your dream— but—but I *am* here. Couldn't you just accept me?"

"No."

The dragon sighed. He floated higher in the air above the pit, crossing his hind legs and resting back on thin air and his long tail. A man-size dragon. "You think I *like* living in this pit?" he demanded mournfully.

"I really hadn't thought about it."

"You're a cruel princess."

"I'm not a princess at all."

"Yes, you are. And you have to kiss me so I'll turn into your prince."

"You've got to be kidding."

A glare was born in the golden eyes. "You're not taking me seriously!"

"Forgive me," she murmured. "It's hard to be serious when conversing with a dragon in a dream."

"It's only partly a dream," he assured her.

"What? What's the other part?"

"Reality." The dragon shrugged. "You see, if I'd appeared as your prince, you wouldn't have accepted me. You're a fighter, you know. Always have been. So I had to come as a dragon."

"That doesn't make sense."

"Of course, it does. I'm the dragon you can't slay. I won't disappear if you fight me. The only way to get rid of me is to kiss me. Then I'll be a prince and not a dragon."

"It seems to me," Brooke said thoughtfully, "that if I turn you into a prince, I'll really be stuck with you."

The dragon looked hurt again. "A *very* cruel princess," he noted sadly.

"I'd like to wake up now," Brooke announced.

"Sorry. Beyond my power. You have to jump."

Brooke stamped a foot. "It's *my* dream and I want to wake up!"

A feathered eyebrow lifted again. He drifted closer, big golden eyes blinking like the mysterious eyes of a cat. "Then kiss me," he said, his voice dropping to a note that was warm and compelling.

Brooke stared at him for a moment, then looked down at the tennis shoes on her slender feet. Speculatively she murmured, "I wonder what would happen if I clicked my heels together three times?"

"You're not in Oz," the dragon scoffed.

She sighed. "I know. I'm in the middle of a really crazy dream talking to a ridiculous dragon who thinks he's the dragon version of a frog-prince."

"Stop talking about frogs," the dragon begged. "It's bad enough being a dragon! C'mon now— don't you want to wake up? Give us a kiss!"

Giggling suddenly Brooke held up a disdainful hand. "Keep your distance, sir!" she commanded, trying to appear regal in jeans and a knit top. "I don't kiss dragons."

The dragon crossed his hind legs the other way and folded the forelegs across his feathered chest. "This is not the way the story was written," he complained. "You're supposed to kiss me."

Before Brooke could respond, he abruptly disappeared down into the pit. She stepped to the bow of the boat, holding on tightly and bending cautiously to look. Blackness.

"Dragon?" she called, hearing her voice echo endlessly. "Dragon, are you there?" It was ridiculous: she felt disappointed. Then her field of vision was filled with golden eyes and golden feathers, and the feathers were brushing her face. Something warm and undragonlike touched her lips.

Chuckling delightedly, the dragon floated back a couple of feet, his clawed forepaws clapping together. "I stole one!" he crowed triumphantly.

"Thief!" Brooke accused, leaning even farther to swipe at him with one hand. The dragon seemed to be shimmering before her eyes, changing somehow. She felt feathers come away in her hand and suddenly she knew that face, recognized it. Then her balance went haywire and she was plunging headfirst over the bow of the boat and into blackness.

"Help!" She heard her own panicked yell and then the dragon's "What the hell?" and he seemed to be calling her name but she was still falling and she couldn't fly with only a handful of feathers and no wings at all. . . .

"Brooke!"

She shot bolt upright in bed, dimly aware of hugging her pillow to her breasts. After the first breathless feeling of returning to reality from a dream, she also became aware that her bedroom light was on and that Cody was sitting on the edge of her bed and staring at her anxiously. On the floor at the other side of her bed was Phantom, braced up on his three good legs and gazing at her as his tail waved rather doubtfully.

Brooke reached up to push tumbled hair off her forehead and produced a glare, which she aimed at Cody. "That wasn't fair!"

He looked bewildered. "*What* wasn't fair?" he demanded a bit unsteadily. "I mean, besides your waking me up in the dead of night screaming something that sounded like 'Thief,' you scared the hell out of me! And then, when I turned the light on, there you were, wrestling with the covers and yelling for help. What in God's name were you dreaming?"

Brooke started to tell him—at length and in great detail—but she started giggling before intelligible words could work their way out. The giggles turned into laughter, fed by the increasing confusion on Cody's face. She hid her own face in the pillow, the entire dream flashing through her mind with the clarity of a movie.

She felt lightheaded, dizzy, and yet strangely free. It was as if her subconscious mind had struggled to resolve some conflict, shrouding it in symbolism and flinging it at her in a dream. And Brooke didn't know why it was so funny, but it was somehow, and even funnier to remember how many emotions she'd been feeling in the past twenty-four hours. A watchful part of her mind wondered idly if she was hysterical, and when she finally lifted her face from the pillow, she saw a suspicion of the same thought on Cody's face.

Before he could administer the traditional remedy, Brooke choked off the laughter and lifted a hand in a wait-a-minute gesture. "I—I'm fine," she managed a bit shakily.

"Are you sure?" he asked, unconvinced. "This is the first time I've ever seen someone wake up from a nightmare and then burst into laughter."

"It—it wasn't really a nightmare."

"No?" Cody reached over to pry her hand loose from the pillow. He held the hand between them for a moment, looking at it, then gazed quizzically back at her. "Then why'd you shred your pillow?"

Brooke looked at the mangled corner of her pillow, then uncurled her fingers and saw that she'd acquired a deathgrip on a handful of feathers. She started to giggle again.

"Hey, don't do that again," Cody begged quickly. "You're making me nervous."

She swallowed the giggles and carefully cleared her throat. "I'm fine, Cody—really. It wasn't a nightmare, just—just a somewhat involved dream. Nothing to worry about."

Cody didn't release her hand. "Are you sure? I thought somebody was killing you. Although who'd come way up here on a night like this . . . ?" He lifted his head as the wail of the wind suddenly penetrated into the room. "It's storming again."

Brooke hastily averted her eyes from his bare and unexpectedly furry chest, trying to ignore the little voice in her head reminding her brightly that she'd never seen his naked chest before. Looking steadfastly at her pillow, she murmured, "I'm sure. And I'll probably sleep just fine now; I always do in a storm."

Cody, having a problem with his own eyes since Brooke was wearing some kind of filmy nylon thing with a plunging V-neckline, rather hastily accepted her assurances. He released her hand and rose to his feet. "Okay, then. But if you have another— involved dream . . ."

"Uh-huh," Brooke murmured quickly, her sidelong glance showing her that Cody wore pajama bottoms. She wondered if he'd been about to offer to keep her company, but she wasn't about to ask. "Good night, Cody."

He crossed the room to the open door, pausing there with one hand on the doorknob and one on the light switch, his glance going to where Phantom had curled himself up on the rug beside Brooke's bed.

Brooke followed his glance. "He won't hurt me, Cody."

"I know." Cody smiled just a little. "After all, he's spent every night in here, hasn't he?" When Brooke only blinked at him, he added softly, "Good night, honey. Sweet dreams." He went out, turning off the light and closing the door.

Brooke sat there for a moment while her eyes adjusted to the darkness, then looked down at the feathers she was still holding. Thoughtfully she leaned over and deposited them on her nightstand. Then she put the wounded pillow at the foot of her bed, drew the covers up, and energetically pounded the other pillow. Before putting her head on it, she peered over the side of the bed and at the wolf quietly lying on the rug.

"Phantom, did you ever hear of the Cinderella Complex?" she asked musingly. The wolf thumped his tail once in polite if sleepy attention. Sighing, Brooke lay back on her pillow and stared at the shadowy ceiling.

"Someday my prince will come," she murmured, and then giggled. "Trust me not to have the traditional human or frog-prince. My prince has to be a talkative feathered dragon!"

Just before she drifted off to sleep, Brooke heard her voice again, the words unconnected with thought.

"I wonder where I landed . . . or if he caught me . . . I wonder if I should have jumped. . . ."

Six

Cody grew more bemused during the following few days. Until then, he'd felt that he possessed a fairly accurate perspective regarding Brooke. He had identified her dragons and fought them the best way he knew how, first with his patience and then in forcing Brooke to face her feelings toward her mother. He didn't doubt that his methods had been successful, because Brooke seemed to have become a different woman overnight.

That was what baffled him.

He'd first been knocked off balance by the fact that she accepted his touch just as casually as ever—but with a new amusement that Cody could sense but not really pinpoint. Her green eyes always invited him to share her amusement, and a puzzled Cody couldn't see the joke. Still, if it had been only that, he could have coped.

It was more than that.

She called him Prince. She teased him in a manner which, Cody felt strongly, was more reminiscent of a lover than a pal—the way she'd teased him until then. She was casually offhand about touching him. There was an expression in her eyes from time to time that touched something primitive deep inside Cody, the expression of a woman becoming aware of her own womanhood. But at the same time she seemed to have discovered the childlike enthusiasm and recklessness that her mother's exploitation had banished.

And it was that childlike, infectious cheerfulness that kept Cody more off-balance than anything else. It made him hesitant, even though his instincts told him that it was time their relationship be clearly defined; either it would grow or it would remain the same. And he had only to feel the casual touch of her hand to know that it couldn't remain the same; not for him.

Cody damned his own uncertainty even while encouraging Brooke's present mood—whatever it was. If she laughed, he egged her on. If she became irritated, he played that up as well. It seemed a promising sign to him that her emotions were closer to the surface now.

But he lay awake in his lonely bed on more than one night brooding over the number of women he'd met since she'd first knocked him into the snow. The unwelcoming, stiffly controlled woman. The terrified woman. The bitter woman. The woman who'd gradually relaxed in his company. The woman lost in painful memories. The woman who'd cried in his arms. The woman who'd laughed almost hysterically after a dream—nightmare? —and looked at a handful of feathers as if they were priceless diamonds.

And now the woman who was none of those others and yet all of them, the woman who laughed and teased and gazed at him with the most beautiful green eyes he'd ever seen, and a smile that could send a man winging to heaven—or plummeting straight to hell. . . .

"Oh, hell!"

Cody looked up, startled. "What?"

She gazed at him with round, innocent eyes. "Nothing."

"I'll never understand women," Cody said with a sigh.

Brooke propped her elbows on the coffee table and on top of the jigsaw puzzle they'd half completed, regarding him with a disquieting look in her eyes. "That remark," she said solemnly, "must have been born when people were still living in caves."

"I wouldn't doubt it."

"It set a bad precedent," Brooke stated firmly. "If some misguided man hadn't said it to his pals, then his descendants would have had to *learn* instead of claiming bewilderment."

Cody stared at her. "I'm willing to be taught," he said wryly.

"Good."

"And so?"

"And so what?"

"Teach me."

Brooke lifted an eyebrow at him. "One step at a time, Prince."

"Then start with that." Cody sat back on the couch and stared at her across the puzzle. "Why d'you keep calling me that?"

"You said it yourself. You said: 'Trust me, lady. I'm a prince.' I decided to trust you."

"But what does it *mean*?" Cody asked ruefully.

Brooke smiled. "That I call you Prince? It means that I trust you, Cody."

He forced himself not to leap at the first thought that crossed his mind—the thought that Brooke was trying to tell him something. Cody had no intention of losing ground through a misunderstanding. "You . . . trust me as a friend?" he inquired cautiously.

She dropped her gaze suddenly to a puzzle piece she was turning in her fingers. "If I were unscrupulous," she murmured evasively, "I'd read your mind instead of sitting here and trying to guess what you're thinking."

"Brooke?" he breathed, abruptly conscious of tension in himself and in the room . . . and in her.

Long lashes hiding her eyes, Brooke continued to toy with the puzzle piece she held. "In all the books," she said almost inaudibly, "this is where the hero snatches the heroine up in his arms and . . ." She laughed softly, unsteadily. "Give him an inch, and he takes a mile. The thing is"—she looked up suddenly—"I'm not sure I'm ready for that mile, Cody. But I wouldn't mind . . . starting the trip."

Brooke listened to the words coming from her own mouth, realizing that she was about to jump into the pit of her own free will and face a dragon that might or might not be a prince. She was afraid and excited and horribly unsure of herself, and damn the man for sitting there as if he were made of stone! Didn't he realize that she'd never tried to seduce a man and didn't have the faintest idea of how to go about it? Didn't he know that she was aching with what had become a familiar pain, something she'd identified as hunger for the golden warmth that was him?

Didn't he understand that she was willingly taking a chance for the first time in years? Couldn't he see that she was shaking and that the heat in her cheeks didn't come from the fire behind her but the one inside her?

And then he must have seen, must have realized, because she was suddenly not kneeling on the bearskin rug anymore—she was lying back on it and he was beside her, and she wondered vaguely what Phantom would do when he came back from the kitchen to find his favorite rug occupied. But it didn't matter. Nothing mattered but the golden eyes blazing down at her with an incandescence she'd never seen before, a smoldering need written in his firelit face and in the arms that drew her close.

"Brooke . . ." One hand smoothed a strand of black hair away from her flushed face, and Cody looked deeply into green eyes that held shy promises he hadn't dared to hope for. He felt as if a fragile and elusive hummingbird had flown trustingly into his grasp, and at that moment he wanted more than anything else in the world not to betray that trust, not to injure a heart with too many scars on it.

He touched her face softly, his fingers tracing the curve of her brows and the clean line of her jaw. He touched her gently, silently promising that he would never demand more of her than she was willing to give, that he would never betray the hard-won trust.

Brooke could feel the assurances in his touch, and the last barrier in her mind crumbled gently into dust. For the first time in years she felt no need for walls, for protection. And his thoughts didn't rush through with the force she was afraid of; they flowed gently, interlacing within her own, until it didn't matter. There was no intrusion, no lack of inner privacy. Somehow, through instinct, intuition, or a form of ESP neither had been aware of, Cody touched her mind without disturbing it.

The loneliness of being locked inside herself lightened slowly, gratitude welling up to replace it. She wasn't alone anymore, and Brooke absorbed the warmth of Cody's presence with wonder. Even her heart seemed to beat with the rhythm of his. She sighed without being aware of it; her hands slid up around his neck, feeling the soft, heavy weight of his golden hair and tangling her fingers in the silky strands.

Only then did Cody's head lower and his mouth find hers. He kissed her as if for the first time: gently, tenderly, his passion held in check by the very depth of his own inner commitment.

But neither Cody nor Brooke was prepared for her instant and total response, and even his commitment and her uncertainty wavered and caught fire in the eruption of sheer desire. A need greater than any Brooke had ever known lanced through her body, beating in her veins with a wild, untamed rhythm. Colors whirled behind her closed eyelids, and the empty ache somewhere deep inside of her grew to fill her being with a hollow, thumping agony.

It was frightening, the depth of her need, but Brooke pushed the fleeting fear aside. A reckless compulsion held her in its grip, and she didn't care anymore that she was jumping into the pit. Cody would catch her; she could trust him to catch her. . . .

Control slipping from his grasp, the kiss deepening far beyond what he'd meant it to be, Cody fought a brief, fleeting battle for sanity—and lost. A groan ripped its way from deep inside him and disappeared with a rumble somewhere in his throat. His mouth slanted across hers hungrily, taking without demand because she was offering everything and he couldn't ask for more than that. All his senses seemed to overload and then explode, a shivering tension sensitizing every nerve in his body.

Brooke felt one of his hands holding the nape of her neck, felt the other hand sliding with a rough warmth beneath her bulky sweater and touching the smooth flesh of her back. She could feel the strength in his hands, and the desire that was unhurried even in its fierce hunger, and her own hands moved to mold the muscles rippling beneath his flannel shirt.

His lips left hers at last to feather hot, fiery kisses down her throat to the V-neckline of her sweater, his hand sliding around to her stomach and then moving slowly up her rib cage. Brooke gasped, biting back a moan when the hand surrounded a swollen breast and the heart pounding beneath it. Her fingers locked in his hair, her body arching into his with a hunger and an instinct older than civilization.

And then a sound jerked them apart, a sound alien in the snowbound quiet of weeks, shocking in its abruptness, and yet incongruously signaling normality. From the end table three feet away, the phone brazenly demanded a response.

Brooke stared up into startled, glazed golden eyes, hearing Cody's harsh breathing rasping in time with her own. Her first thought was that somebody had lousy timing, and even in the disappointment of interruption, a giggle bubbled in her throat. "I thought this only happened in bad novels," she managed in a husky voice.

"*Damn* that thing!" Cody muttered, but his eyes

were lightening with reluctant amusement. "Can't get away from it even in the back of beyond."

The phone pealed demandingly.

"I don't think they're going to hang up," Brooke said.

Cody bent his head to kiss her lingeringly. "No. No, I suppose not. Want me to get it?"

She unlocked her fingers slowly, letting them glide along his jaw before falling away. Sighing, she murmured, "I guess you'd better."

With obvious reluctance Cody got to his feet and went over to pick up the receiver, silencing the maddening ring. Brooke sat up and ran her fingers through her long hair, watching him and not giving a particular damn who was on the phone.

Phantom appeared in the doorway, ears pointed, eyes keen.

"Hello?"

Even from three feet away, Brooke heard what sounded like the roaring of a very big bear from the bottom of a very deep well. And the voice erupted with such noisy violence that Cody immediately jerked the receiver a good five inches away from his ear.

Watching his face, Brooke saw the initial astonishment blend into brief bemusement and then a growing and unholy amusement. He tried several times to break into the flow of narrative, but finally just listened with a grin. Five minutes later, the definitely one-sided call over, Cody sank down on the couch and proceeded to laugh himself silly.

Brooke, whether through the tenuous contact with him or through inspired guesswork, had identified the caller. She noted that Phantom padded away as she waited for Cody to show signs of getting himself under control before exclaiming, "Wasn't that Thor? Has Pepper . . .?"

Cody wiped streaming eyes. "Pepper has," he gasped. "Twins. Boy and girl. And the proud papa is a two-hundred-pound nervous breakdown!"

Brooke had met Thor only once, some months earlier during a brief visit, and a vision of that very large and very self-possessed man rose before her eyes. He'd seemed endearingly fascinated and bemused by his lively wife, clearly head-over-heels in love with her, but hardly the type of man to fall apart at the seams for any reason.

"Do we know the same man?" Brooke asked uncertainly. "I didn't think anything could shake him."

"That's what's so funny!" Cody made a determined effort to control his amusement. "Thor *isn't* the kind of man to be easily shaken—although I could tell the last time I talked to Pepper that he was beginning to fray around the edges."

"Well, what did he say?" Brooke asked, rising and moving to sit on the couch beside Cody. "Is Pepper all right?"

Cody slipped an arm around her shoulders. "Pepper's fine; the babies are fine." He chuckled. "But I'm not sure that Thor even knew who he was talking to. He roared that it was twins, boy and girl, then bellowed that they weighed exactly six pounds each. Then he bawled something about hostages, asked if I wanted a cigar, and rapidly went into an unintelligible tailspin. I've never heard a man sound so deliriously terrified!"

Brooke started to laugh. "Did he mention names for the babies?"

"If he did, they didn't make sense. I hope to God Pepper can calm him down before he goes completely to pieces; if he was calling from the hospital, they've probably already got him under restraints or sedated!"

Giggling, trying to imagine Thor coming unglued, Brooke said, "Well, at least he isn't blasé about it the way so many men seem to be."

Cody choked back a last laugh. "I know, but there has to be a middle ground!" His arm tightening around her, he added dryly, "As soon as Thor recovers from the shock, I'll have to think of some way to get even with him."

"For what?"

"The interruption."

Brooke looked at him, smiling. "You can't hold him responsible, really. He couldn't have known."

Cody's free hand lifted to touch her cheek lightly. "I suppose not. But he certainly broke the mood, didn't he?"

"Maybe that wasn't such a bad thing," she whispered.

His face went very still. "Second thoughts?" he asked quietly.

She shook her head. "No. But it—happened awfully fast, Cody. And I've never felt anything like that before."

"Neither have I."

"No?" She looked at him a little shyly.

"No." His golden eyes were very direct, very honest. "I love you, Brooke."

She caught her breath, wondering why the words should shock her as if he'd never spoken them before. "You seem so certain," she murmured. "So *sure*. How do you know, Cody?"

Smiling, Cody reached over to slide an arm beneath her knees, lifting her easily until she lay across his lap. Holding her close, resting his chin on the top of her head, he mused silently for a moment. "How do I know? You ask tough questions, lady."

Brooke toyed absently with one of the buttons on

his flannel shirt, content to wait for his answer. She needed to hear it, because the abandoned emotions that had raced through her demanded a definition, and she was more than a little afraid to call them love.

After a moment Cody spoke slowly, his tone sober and yet curiously evocative of the deepest emotions. He spoke as if to a third person, weaving the delicate fabric of an elusive yet heartfelt story

"I met a lady one cold night. She was more beautiful than any dream of beauty I'd ever known, and she was wounded—a part of her hiding away and hurting. And I . . . wanted to take away the hurt. I wanted to hear her distant little voice shimmer with laughter. I wanted to see her lovely face light up with warmth and happiness.

" 'I knew it was love and I felt it was glory,' " he quoted softly. "That was the feeling. And her dragons were mine; I had to fight them just as I have to breathe. There was never a choice, never a moment when I could have turned away. Because I loved her.

"The days passed, and I tried to prove to her that she could trust me. She'd been hurt so badly, and I didn't want anything to ever hurt her again. I wanted to show her how much I needed her, but I was afraid of frightening her. So I waited. And the dragons were faced and fought, and the sound of her laughter was like music. And I loved her more.

"When she turned to me finally, reached out for me, I couldn't believe it. I craved her touch, hungered for her smile, and the need I felt for her was a growing, living thing inside of me." Cody hesitated, then finished softly, "Because I loved her."

Brooke lifted her head slowly and stared at him, moved, astonished. There were no longer barriers in her mind, but there existed one around her heart that not even his moving words could completely penetrate. She was afraid to love, almost afraid to *be* loved, and she didn't know why.

Swallowing hard, she murmured huskily, "The wounds are . . . healing. But I need time, Cody. Time to know how I feel. Time to fight . . . one last dragon."

He surrounded her face with warm hands. "Then we'll take the time." Golden eyes smiled at her. "And we'll fight the dragon together." He kissed her very gently.

Not for the world would Brooke have hurt him by telling him that she had to fight the last dragon alone.

Hearts and minds, walls and dragons—and an elusive something called love. Did she love Cody? Brooke didn't know. That he had awakened desire within her she knew; instinct told her that no other man would ever touch her so deeply in that way. Was that love? Was her fierce, constant, maddening need to touch him love?

Was it love that made the sound of his deep voice run along her nerve endings like shimmering fire? Was it love that drew her eyes to him continually? Was it love that had given birth to the bubble of happy laughter she felt all the time now?

Or was all that only a result of defeating the dragon—her mother—that had tormented her entire life in one way or another?

Brooke sorted and sifted and tried to understand. She'd been hurt too many times in her own life ever to willingly hurt another human being; God knew she didn't want to hurt Cody. But she would never again allow herself to accept a situation simply because she craved approval or love, or feared to hurt.

This time, she vowed determinedly, she'd know her mind and her emotions. This time she wouldn't hide from herself as well as from others. She'd have no more dragons rearing their heads to frighten or bewilder or cause pain. Brooke Kennedy was going to take control of her life once and for all.

She had thought playfully of dragons and princes after her dream, even going so far as to thoroughly enjoy Cody's baffled reaction to being called Prince. But that flare of brief and childlike mischief had disappeared in the white-hot blaze of a man's desire igniting her own.

It wasn't a game. They weren't playing Let's Pretend or living in a fairy tale.

At the same time something told Brooke that somehow she could combine both the warmth of her just discovered childhood and her newly blooming womanhood in Cody's presence. He had the ability, she realized dimly, to appreciate and understand both. He could pet and encourage the child while never losing sight of the woman.

That realization warmed her, but it confused her as well. Part of her wanted to *be* the child because she'd never had the chance to be one. But a larger part of her desperately needed to become the whole and complete woman she saw reflected in Cody's wonderful golden eyes.

Alone, Brooke sat on the couch with her feet tucked underneath her and watched the fire she'd just built up. They had turned in for the night hours ago, but she had gotten up again and crept in here to think. And she smiled a little as she remembered how Cody had sensitively and deliberately kept things light between them. He'd left her at her door with a gentle kiss, demanding neither answers nor explanations.

A remarkable man.

Someday her prince would come. . . . Brooke knew that the Cinderella Complex was probably a valid theory, and that many women, conditioned by too many years of romantic expectations, believed at some level of themselves that their princes would, indeed, come. Handsome princes on the modern equivalent of a white charger, sweeping them off their feet in a breathless rush of romance and carrying them to Happily-Ever-After-Land.

Cheated out of her girlish childhood by reality and denied daydreams by the control she'd been forced to exert over her own mind, Brooke knew that she herself had never indulged, even unconsciously, in fantasies. She'd never craved the "rescue" of a prince because there had been no child deep inside of her to create him. Hard reality had matured her swiftly, wrapping her in a shell of loneliness and confusion, and then layering over that with bitterness and pain.

So Brooke had no real conception of the happily-ever-after dream. Day-to-day living she understood and accepted; disappointment and unhappiness she knew to be a part of life. If one were lucky, she'd come to realize, then a careful balance between happiness and unhappiness could be achieved; if there were no great expectations, there would be no great disappointments.

And she was confused and afraid now because Cody had turned her smooth balance into something entirely different. There were high peaks and low valleys now, and the beginnings of expectations so great that they terrified her. A child locked away and hidden inside of her had been freed, and had dared to dream of a prince.

Disappointment. She'd lived with it her entire life, watched it tangle with grief and loss. She was older more from experience than years. Older from loss. Loss of illusions, of ideals. Loss of a childhood barely begun. Loss of those she loved, or had wanted to love.

She couldn't bear to lose again.

Cody, the golden man, the stuff of princes. He'd come into her life just ahead of a blizzard, the innate warmth of him contrasting dizzily with the cold winter and her cold loneliness. He'd come and said that he loved her, and had demanded before realizing that demands were blows from a punishing fist to her. Demands had bowed to patience, and he had taught her to trust him. To trust him . . . and perhaps to love him, but she couldn't love him, couldn't be loved by him, because—

She couldn't bear to lose again.

Brooke sighed raggedly, barely seeing Phantom's ears twitch at the sound as he lifted his head from the bearskin rug and looked at her alertly.

That was it, then. The final dragon, the beast looming to block off her future. She couldn't bear to lose again. She could, she thought, trust Cody not to leave her, but she couldn't trust life not to take him away from her. And she couldn't trust herself not to strangle him with her own fear if she let herself accept that she loved him.

She heard herself laughing, a dull and unamused laugh. The last dragon, and not all the magic swords ever dreamed could slay it. It loomed mockingly in front of her, daring her to love and lose. It tormented her, because its golden eyes held the promises she'd seen in Cody's eyes. And the newly awakened child-woman who'd dared to dream of a prince and conceive of happily-ever-after felt the familiar sting of reality and the bitter taste of disappointment.

His voice came quietly into the firelit room, warm and gentle and as achingly familiar as bitterness and defeat.

"Slaying dragons all alone in the dark?" Cody asked, coming around the end of the couch to sit down beside her. He was wearing a dark robe belted over pajama bottoms, his golden hair a little tumbled.

Brooke absently tightened the tie-belt of her own quilted robe, looking at him and wanting desperately to go on looking at him because it fed something ravenously hungry inside of her. "Leave," she said suddenly, almost inaudibly. "Go away, Cody—far away. I'm not good for you."

Half turned to face her, resting an elbow on the back of the couch, Cody lifted a hand to trace the distinctive widow's peak high on her forehead. He was clearly undismayed by her abrupt words. "Why don't you let me be the judge of that," he said softly.

She shook her head a little. "I—I don't think you're very objective," she told him.

He smiled. "And you are?"

"Yes." Brooke gazed at him—direct, honest, her green eyes very clear and fathoms deep. "Right now, at this moment, I am objective. Right now I can tell you to leave."

"Right now," he responded, "I can't leave. Since that first night there's never been a moment when I could have. And there never will be, Brooke."

Brooke looked at him steadily, the moment of objectivity passing. Her green eyes clouded, becoming opaque. He wouldn't leave, and she'd never again be able to ask him to leave. "I'm not good for you," she repeated painfully.

His hand slid down beneath the heavy weight of her hair to cup her neck gently. "What is it, honey?" he asked quietly. "What's that dragon been whispering to you here in the dark?"

In a low voice, apparently going off on a tangent, Brooke answered his question with a question. "How old were you, Cody, when you realized that the world was bigger than you knew, and colder? How old were you when you—put away childish things and realized what reality meant?"

He answered her soberly. "I was older than most—in my twenties. A close friend lost his parents, and I saw what it did to him."

"Thor," she guessed, knowing the two men had grown up together.

Cody nodded. "Thor."

Brooke was silent for a moment, thinking about the depth of this man, his sensitivity and understanding. She never ceased to marvel at his generosity of spirit, the luxuriant warmth of him. It was always unexpected, because Cody looked like a breaker of hearts, his face full of the handsomeness women endowed their dream princes with; but there was layer after layer of him, each one showing more of the innate wisdom and understanding that a much older man would have envied.

"How about you?" he asked, knowing what the answers would be.

She looked into the flickering fire. "Six," she murmured. "And ten. Have you ever lost something that mattered to you, Cody?"

Cody looked at her, at the beautiful profile, and something as old as the cave lurched inside of him. He knew that there was a part of this woman he wouldn't be able to touch even after years of knowing her; a scarred and lonely part of her that could never be revealed in mere words because the hurt had gone so deep.

"No. I've been lucky." He heard the choked sound of his own voice, and knew that the lump in his throat was born out of fear.

She had sat here in the dark and fought a dragon alone, and Cody realized then that she'd lost the battle. It didn't matter somehow that other battles had been fought and won; it mattered only that the silent battle in this firelit darkness had been lost. There was something between them now, something that hadn't been there before. It was a chasm—he on one side and she on the other—and she wouldn't help him to build a bridge. For some reason she'd made up her mind that there wouldn't be a bridge.

"You see?" she said very quietly. "I'm not good for you."

Cody thought at first that she was referring to his answers being so different from hers that she was giving the chasm a name. But then he realized that she was looking at him again, that she'd seen some reaction in his face that he hadn't been able to control.

"Look what I'm doing to you, Cody."

"What are you doing?" he asked tautly, wishing that he'd come into the room sooner; wishing that she hadn't come to the decision that was making his heart pound sickly in his chest.

"Hurting you," she answered bleakly. Her hands locked tightly together on her thighs, the knuckles whitening.

It sounded like good-bye, like the beginning of good-bye, and Cody realized then that he'd walk barefoot through hell itself, fighting dragons, devils, and demons to prevent good-bye. The fleeting thought of a life without her was an emptiness that struck him a physical blow.

"No," he said, denying that brief vision rather than her words.

The opacity of her eyes hurt him. The dull remoteness of her voice hurt him. The chasm lying between them like the toothless grin of a mocking devil hurt him. It hurt him that there was a part of her he might never be able to touch, might never know, even if he somehow managed to bridge the chasm.

With an odd little cry she suddenly reached out to him, her arms going blindly around his neck, her face against his shoulder, her voice muffled. "Oh, don't! Don't look like that," she pleaded. "I don't want to hurt you; don't let me hurt you!"

His arms went just as blindly around her, holding her to assure himself of the reality of flesh and bone. He felt her heart thudding in time with his own, and it still wasn't enough. The fear of losing her was suddenly so strong that he would have done anything, sacrificed anything, for the certainty of never losing her.

Cody had never felt so shaken, so desperate. This wasn't a matter of physical desire; it was a feeling so crucial, a need so imperative that it defied description, refused the flimsy label of words. The steadily building emotions he'd grappled with during the past weeks paled next to what he was feeling then. Always strong, always able to cope with life and with himself, he felt parts of himself never exposed until then open up suddenly, and they were achingly empty because she wasn't there.

It was a madness just as violent, just as all-consuming as the passion they'd shared earlier.

But this madness, this berserk need, was in his mind and his heart. He heard his voice, a rough and grating sound, and knew that the words were welling up from that madness, from that wild place deeper than conscious thought; knew that the words spoke a truth more basic than his conscious mind would ever know or understand.

"I won't lose you . . . can't lose you . . . darling . . . my darling . . . nothing matters but you . . . nothing makes sense but you . . . there's no peace without you . . . no life. . . . I love you . . . I need you . . . so badly . . . I've loved you forever . . . even before I knew you . . . Brooke . . . my beautiful, hurt Brooke . . . I'm yours more than my own. . . ."

Seven

Brooke heard his words, heard them with her mind and her heart. She heard the sound of raw truth. She heard a winging wildness and vulnerability, and a soaring need unbridled by the trappings of civilized man. She heard a love so powerful, so basic and essential that it shook her as nothing had ever shaken her in her life.

Not even a dragon could stand against it.

The fear was still present, hovering around the edges of consciousness, demanding a confrontation. But she didn't try to confront it then. There would be time for that, she knew. Time to discover if she'd been caught up in his madness because it *was* his madness, or because she shared it. Time to hear what price she might pay for the chance she was taking. Time to regret, if regrets there would be.

But in that moment she jumped into the pit,

eyes wide open and fully aware of the action. Dragon or prince, she was bound to Cody in some manner she couldn't fully comprehend, could only accept. It was more than love, more than love knew how to be, and she embraced it and welcomed it because there was nothing else she could do.

Her fingers tangled in his thick hair, she raised her head and looked at him, seeing even through the blur of her tears that his eyes, his beautiful golden eyes, were dim and distant, still in that stark place where the truth had been wrenched from.

"Cody . . . I love you, Cody," she whispered, wanting to shout it, wanting to sing it, but unable to force more than the whisper past the huge lump in her throat that might have been her heart. "I love you. . . ."

His eyes cleared, warmed, blazed suddenly with the fire she only then recognized as hers. A sound rumbled in his throat, escaped in a choked groan of relief, of delight. He kissed her with an urgency just this side of savagery, his passion the rare kind not of the flesh but of the spirit.

Brooke responded wholeheartedly, sighing with contentment when he pulled her down on the cushions until they lay close together. "I love you," she murmured, her head on his shoulder. The hard strength of his body was an anchor in the wind, and she nestled to its warmth with a feeling of coming home.

"I love you," he whispered, his voice as exhausted as her own, as drained by emotion. And there was contentment there, the sound of a man at peace.

The fire in the hearth was long-dead ashes when

sunlight began to crawl across the hardwood floor toward the couch. It crept slowly, its brightness waking Phantom momentarily. The wolf lifted his head long enough to see that his humans were still sleeping, then he returned to warm dreams of a summer valley and his sleek and canny mate.

The light crept on.

It shimmered brightly on the glass-topped coffee table, began climbing determinedly up the couch.

Cody felt the light and heat, turning his head away automatically as his eyes drifted open. He saw Brooke's sleep-vulnerable face nestled close, saw her hand resting trustingly on his chest. She smelled of a curious spicy cinnamon scent that was Brooke, and he gazed into her face intently, trying to memorize what it would take a lifetime to know. . . .

Brooke was dreaming.

She was back with the dragon again, after the dizzying ride through the huge whirlpool, and she was sitting at the bow of her little boat, unworried this time by the possibility of falling into the pit. That first fall, the dragon had assured her, was the worst. It took only a little practice, he predicted, and she'd be quite good at it.

He was floating just a foot or so away from her, his undragonlike face frowning slightly because they were disagreeing again. "You've fallen once and jumped once," he reminded her sternly. "And you still won't kiss me?"

With all the gravity he could have wished for Brooke tried to make him understand what was still hazy to herself. "It's not that easy. Admitting that I love is one thing, but I'm still afraid."

"What's to be afraid of?" he asked reasonably. "People fall in love and have lives together. You know—the pitter-patter of little feet, a mongrel dog, and a mortgage?"

Brooke frowned at him. "You're not people," she pointed out.

"I will be when you kiss me."

She frowned harder. "That's just it—you won't be. I mean, I'm not so sure you're real. I'm nervous of extremes in anything, and you're just a little too good to be true. If you're who you're supposed to be, that is, and I must say that you could look a little more like him if you tried." This last was said irritably.

"Kiss me and I'll look exactly like him," the dragon promised, ignoring the rest.

Brooke folded her arms and glared at him. "You're not listening to me."

"You aren't saying anything that matters."

"It matters to me!" she almost yelled. "I can't lose again, especially not *him*. I'd die if I lost him, that's what scares me. There's no going back now, I know that, but can't you promise that I won't lose him?"

"You know better than that," the dragon chided gently. "I don't have the power to make that kind of promise, and I wouldn't even if I could."

She was startled, then angry. "Dammit, why wouldn't you if you could?"

"Only children expect blind promises."

"I'm not a child! I—"

"Aren't you?" The dragon floated nearer, huge golden eyes very grave and too perceptive. "Aren't you asking me to make the same promise you asked your father for when you were five?"

Brooke wanted to rise, wanted to leave, or wake up, or lash out at him, but she was frozen, numbly listening.

"He promised he'd never leave you, didn't he? But he left, and never mind that it wasn't willingly.

A child couldn't see that. He left you. And your mother left you, although in a different way. And then Josh left you. He didn't promise that he wouldn't; he was too sensible for that. But he left you in the end. And now you want promises from me, empty promises."

"Not empty," she whispered. "It's just that I'm afraid—"

The dragon snorted gently, floating nearer until his golden eyes almost filled her field of vision. "That excuse lacks even the saving grace of orginality, my girl. You're afraid! That's the child in you, crying because the room's dark and there might be a monster in the corner. The woman in you knows that that's unlikely—not impossible, mind you, but unlikely. The woman in you knows that all she has to do is get up and turn on a light, and we both know that's better than lying in the dark and crying over what's quite probably an empty and innocent corner."

Brooke tried to think, tried to understand. "But I can't light up every corner now," she said. "I can't look ahead into all the future corners and make sure they don't have monsters in them. Is that what you mean?"

"That's part of it."

"What's the rest?" she pleaded helplessly. "Please, I'm so afraid!"

The dragon shook his head sadly. "The woman knows. Talk to the woman. Being a child is fine if you want to do childish things, but only a woman can love a man the way he needs to be loved. The child can make him laugh and touch his heart—but only the woman can *hold* his heart."

The dragon began sinking slowly into the pit.

Questions raced through Brooke's mind. "Wait!" she cried, leaning over the bow to stare into the black pit. "At least tell me how many times I have to jump into this pit!"

The dragon's voice, wryly amused, floated up to her. "As many times as it takes—until you get it right. Now, jump! He was always there to catch you, you know. Always."

Brooke fell more than jumped, and it occurred to her vaguely as she tumbled through warm darkness that at this rate she'd never learn how to do the thing right. . . .

At some point she seemed to stop falling and start rising, and before she could be confused about that the dream was only a clear memory and she was awake.

He was there beside her, the arms around her warm and strong, and Brooke felt her love for him bubbling inside of her; there wasn't enough room within her to hold it all, but that was all right. Everything was all right. She pushed the fear away, pushed it into the pit and left it for dreams. Dream conversations with the absurd dragon seemed to be dulling the edges of the fear anyway.

"Good morning, love," Cody murmured, his golden eyes bright and smiling.

Brooke lifted her face for his kiss, feeling the steady beat of his heart beneath her hand. "I love you," she told him solemnly, because it seemed she hadn't said it enough, could never say it enough.

Cody framed her face in his hands, drinking in the look that satisfied a hunger deep inside of him. "I love you too, honey. So much. So very much." He was just about to demonstrate when a polite—if badly timed—nudge informed them that their houseguest wanted his breakfast and his morning outing.

Laughing, they disentangled themselves and got up from the couch.

"If you'll feed him while I get dressed," Brooke said, "I'll take him out afterward."

"Deal," Cody said, his eyes caressing her.

Nature decided that the day called for sleet, so she spread an icy coating over the deep snow outside. The weather bulletin on the radio dolefully predicted more of the same for days and observed that the larger part of Montana looked to be snowed-in for the winter.

Mister suddenly rebelled against his self-imposed captivity when Brooke went to feed him, charging out of the barn for all of two feet before halting with a comical look of surprise on his faded gray face when he encountered a snowdrift as high as his chest. Showing the patiently waiting Brooke a yellow-toothed grimace to prove he was still in charge, the old burro worked himself out of the snowbank with dignity and went back inside to the comfort of his straw-lined stall.

And Phantom surprised both Brooke and Cody by breaking his familiar silence. Asking to go outside twice that day, he disappeared around the corner of the lodge as usual for a few minutes, then returned to the back. Once there, he halted several yards away from the back door, gazed off toward the mountain peaks that were barely visible in the driving sleet, then turned his muzzle to the sky and howled mournfully.

When it happened that morning, the eerie sound brought Cody quickly back from his bedroom. He found Brooke at the back door, staring out at the wolf.

"What the hell?" Cody muttered, coming up behind her and putting his arms around her.

Brooke shook her head slightly. "I don't know. Look—he seems to be listening. D'you suppose he's calling Psyche?"

Phantom howled again

Cody rested his chin against her hair. "Could be. He's gained back most of the weight he lost and the leg's nearly healed. I wonder if she'll come back for him; the hunting can't be great around here with this weather."

They remained motionless, watching the wolf. He howled once more, seemed to listen again, then turned back for the lodge. If he was dejected, only Phantom knew; to the watching humans his behavior was exactly the same. They dried him off, and he lay down on the rug by the kitchen fire with his accustomed rumbling growl.

His human caretakers looked at each other, both of them hoping silently that Phantom's mate would return. Someday.

It was an odd day, very quiet inside the lodge, very contented. Companionable from the first, Brooke and Cody discovered that last night's emotional storm had left them more attuned than ever. It was love, but it was more than that, and both were willing to take the time and explore the feelings. And if there was an undercurrent of the strong physical desire that had surprised them both, a spark with every touch, that was fine, too, and worth taking the time to savor.

There was no need to rush.

They talked about pasts. Brooke finished her story, telling Cody how her uncle Josh had heard about the mentalist "shows" through a friend and, horrified at his niece's life, launched a court battle for legal custody of the sixteen-year-old. About the eight peaceful years with Josh. About the second court battle four years ago when her vengeful mother had reappeared in her life and tried to wrest Brooke's inheritance from her after Josh's death. About her mother's death two years ago.

The story was painful for Brooke to recount, but her bitterness seemed to have melted away. Taking its place was only sadness, a sadness that Cody intuitively understood.

"She died before things could be . . . resolved," he murmured, looking up at Brooke. He was lying with his head in her lap, and she gazed down at him with a smile.

"Part of me wanted to confront her with what she'd done to me; I never did that, you know. Never said a word to her. But now I'm almost—glad that I didn't confront her. I can't love her, can't respect her, but I'm glad that the guilt of—hasty words won't haunt me."

Cody held her hand tightly. "I'm glad too. And I'm glad that dragon's been fought."

Her green eyes left memory behind and lightened in amusement. "Thanks to a certain dragonslaying prince."

He smiled modestly. "Think nothing of it, ma'am. Happy to oblige."

Brooke laughed suddenly. "Well, finally! I didn't think I'd ever hear a Texas accent from you, but that was pure drawl."

Cody winced. "I tried to get rid of that accent."

"I think it sounds sweet," Brooke said consideringly.

" 'I love you' sounds sweeter," he murmured.

She bent her head to kiss him, the electricity arcing between them more powerful with this kiss than the last, growing as it had been growing all day, leaving breath a bit ragged and hearts thudding erratically.

Brooke looked down at him, the empty ache throbbing inside of her. The tawny fire in his eyes beckoned, called to her, and at the core of the fire was the love that astonished her.

"You've been very patient with me," she murmured, smoothing back the lock of golden hair from his forehead.

He caught her hand, held it to his cheek. "I love you, Brooke," he said softly.

She smiled just a little, but her voice was unsteady. "I'd forgotten what any kind of love felt like. And this . . . I didn't know it existed. I didn't know I could feel like this. Do you realize what you've done for me, Cody?"

"What have I done?" he asked gently.

Brooke groped for words. "You've—freed me. I've felt like a—a prisoner inside myself for years; I don't feel that way now. And my own mind isn't my enemy anymore."

"I'm glad."

"I love you, Cody." Before he could respond, she added distractedly, "That's not enough, somehow it's not enough just to say that!"

"I know." He was smiling, his golden eyes darkening to sweet honey. "I feel the same way. Words aren't enough."

She looked down at him, and suddenly, like the words, savoring her feelings just wasn't enough. Her mind flew back to the night before and Cody's stark vulnerability; he'd shown her his love, stripped bare for her a part of himself she knew no one else would ever see. Not mere words invented by man, but the raw and frenzied emotions themselves.

No—words weren't enough. Words would never be enough. . . .

Cody sat up and turned to face her on the couch, puzzled by her sudden stillness, by the distant green eyes. And then she gazed at him, and the green eyes weren't distant anymore; they were bottomless and greener than green could ever be, and they reached out toward his soul.

"Brooke . . ." he breathed, feeling a quickening, a breathless suspension of every muscle and nerve in his body.

She touched his face as if she were blind, tracing the handsome planes and angles with fingers that quivered. Deep, deep inside her, in that wild place where fires had raged since his first touch, the flames scorched walls holding them captive, demanding release. Brooke leaned forward slowly until her lips met his, her eyes gazing into his, watching them blaze. Then her eyes drifted closed.

And she loosed the fire.

His arms went around her blindly, fiercely, responding to the need in himself and in her. There was no restraint, no caution or hesitation, no uncertainty. There was only desperate need, the mutual reaching for something violently, compulsively *necessary* to them both.

Lips still imprisoned, Brooke dimly felt herself floating, the arms that had lifted a two-hundred-pound wolf holding her as if she weighed nothing. She tangled her fingers in his thick hair, a hunger beyond thought, beyond reason, building toward the critical point. And she gave herself up to it completely, allowing its turbulence to snap the gossamer threads of reality.

Neither of them noticed the wolf lying on the hearth as he raised his head and watched with yellow eyes the man carry the woman from the room. And neither of them heard the almost human sigh as Phantom lowered his head again to the bearskin rug. Adjusting his splinted leg more comfortably, the wolf drifted off to sleep.

Cody carried Brooke into her bedroom without conscious thought. The room was dimly lit by the fire he'd built only an hour before in the hearth, its flickering flames warming, casting shadows. He set her gently on her feet by the turned-down bed, his fingers going immediately to the back zipper of the caftan she'd changed into after supper.

Brooke, her eyes still closed, felt his lips rain warm kisses over her face, her throat. Absently she stepped out of and kicked aside her slippers, going up on tiptoe to fit herself more firmly against his hard body. She heard a faint whisper of sound, felt cool air against the flesh of her back, and then the warmth of his touch was chasing away the chill.

Frantically she found the buttons of his flannel shirt by touch alone, desperate to have no more barriers between them. Her eyes opened at last as he released her long enough to shrug the shirt off, and her own hunger doubled, tripled, erupted, as green eyes met gold.

There was a sudden stillness, an abrupt cessation of all movement. Only eyes touched and probed; even their harsh breathing seemed to have stilled. They gazed at each other for a timeless moment, the crackle of the fire in the hearth a tame thing compared to that winging in human eyes. And then the spell shattered and they reached for each other with one mind.

Brooke was only dimly aware of clothing falling to the floor and kicked aside, hardly conscious of being lifted again and placed on the bed. The covers were pushed aside as Cody joined her, his eyes flitting hungrily over her fire-golden body

"Oh, God, you're beautiful," he rasped, the sound raw and torn from his throat. "Brooke . . . my Brooke. . . ."

Green eyes as enigmatic as those of a cat stared into his, the siren song within them again reaching for his soul, calling to him. He saw the wildness there—the unleashed, uncontrolled, soaring urgency of need stripped bare, and the breath caught in his throat harshly. "Brooke . . ."

"I love you," she whispered, her fingers touching his face again blindly. "I love you, Cody!"

His lips hot and shaking, he kissed her hand, her shoulder, her throat. Her skin was satin beneath his touch, satin inflamed. "I love you," he murmured jerkily, his heart beating so hard and fast that it was a drum roll inside his chest. He couldn't stop touching her, never wanted to stop; he was aching for her.

Brooke felt his hands caressing, learning her, and her own hands searched out and molded the rippling muscles of his back and shoulders. Feverishly, her breath coming in little gasps, she touched him and touched him because it fed the fire inside of her. And then his hands and mouth found the pointed need of her breasts, and a moan jerked from her.

A fiery, shivering tension spread outward from some central core within her, its ripple effect sending wave after wave along her nerves. She couldn't breathe, couldn't move, and then she had to move because she couldn't be still. She felt his tongue swirling erotically around the bud his mouth held captive, the starving hunger of him branding her forever.

His caresses slid lower, lower still, lips following the fiery trail blazed by his hands, and some dim and distant part of Brooke wondered if she'd died, because, she told herself, she couldn't be feeling this, it wasn't possible to feel this and not die of the sheer pleasure of it. There couldn't be more, but there was, and she wanted to beg him to stop, to never stop, because she was dying; the frantic pounding of her heart was smothering her and she was burning from head to toe.

She heard a stranger's breathless voice calling to him, pleading wildly, and the stranger's body moved restlessly with a need too great to bear. His face was taut as he rose above her, another stranger because she'd never seen that face before. But it was fascinating, riveting, that face, because it held imperative need, essential hunger, and love was blazing savagely in two golden fires that threatened to consume her.

There was a moment, a split second during which sanity lowered the flames in those eyes, when awareness sought to find gentleness in the act of possession. Brooke saw that moment, was moved by it, but the primitive woman unleashed with the fire was wildness incarnate.

Fiercely she caught him within herself, branding him as hers, the brief shock of possession an answer to her body's craving.

And the moment for gentleness was gone, dissolved, consumed by rampaging need. It built within them, compelled them, drove them as moths to a flame to burn in a glorious death. They were stripped of everything but that need, their souls laid bare by it, their deepest selves revealed to each other. And they were lost . . . and found . . . and lost again. . . .

The firelit room might have been the eye of a hurricane, and the two shipwrecked survivors clung to each other with the breathless feeling of having gone through something no human had been meant to survive. They held one another as anchors, as lodestones. Drained, they rested together, conscious of the dimly terrifying sensation of having shared an experience too vast to ever forget.

There were no words at first, no thoughts. Only an instinctive and overpowering wonder needing no expression. Not even sleep could claim exhausted bodies or ease stunned minds.

And then for a while there were murmurs not especially noteworthy for their originality or sense. Murmurs of love, murmurs using the inadaquate language of words that could never express the depth of what they felt but helped them to find solid ground again. Until finally they were back, they were themselves once more, the bond between them forged in fire and cooled now to something stronger than either of them.

"Wildcat," Cody whispered, somehow managing to pull the covers up around them without losing his possessive hold on her.

Brooke decided it was a compliment. "Thank you," she murmured, wondering idly how she'd ever managed to rest all these years without the comfort of his shoulder pillowing her head.

"I may never move again," he added, yawning hugely.

She traced an intricate pattern in the hair on his chest, fascinated by the way the firelight glinted off the golden strands. "We'll starve," she said finally, thoughtfully.

"There is that," he agreed.

Silence.

"Cody?"

"Hmm?"

"Will you respect me in the morning?"

Caught in the middle of another yawn, Cody choked on a laugh. "Oh, I'll try," he responded, chuckling.

"I was just wondering," she explained.

"Being inexperienced in these matters?" he asked politely.

"Something like that."

"Mmm. Well, I'll respect any woman who knocks me flat on my back, love," he said, adding, "In the snow, no less."

"You're never going to let me forget that, are you?"

"Of course not."

"Why?"

"I have to keep you in your place, don't I?" he asked, aggrieved.

Brooke wound golden hair around a finger and tugged sharply. "And just what is my place?"

"Ouch." He sighed. "Undiplomatic of me, wasn't it?"

"To say the least."

"Sorry. Uh—maybe I should have said—"

"What?"

"I'm thinking."

"A very wise person said once that if you have to think about it, you aren't going to answer honestly."

"Who said that?"

"Me."

"Oh."

"Well?"

"Let's strike my ill-advised remark from the record, shall we? We'll pretend I didn't say it."

"I don't think I should pretend that."

"Please?"

"Stop sounding pitiful."

"Didn't work, huh?"

"I know you better than that."

"Ah. Well, then—why don't I just apologize?"

"You can try."

"My darling Brooke, I'm desperately sorry I made that stupid, sexist remark. Forgive me?"

"I'll think it over."

"Hell."

"You don't get nothin' for free, pal."

"I'll have to remember those deathless words," he said thoughtfully.

Brooke punched him weakly in the ribs.

Cody retaliated by patting her gently on the fanny.

She giggled in spite of herself. "Such a gentleman."

"Always."

Brooke snuggled closer to him, the love so near to the surface now washing over her in a tidal wave. "I love you," she told him fiercely.

His arms tightened around her. "I love you too, darling," he said softly, intensely.

"Forever?" Her voice was unconsciously wistful.

"Forever," he vowed deeply.

Brooke saw the last dragon rear its head before her, and slammed the door against it before it could destroy her newfound happiness. Later, she told herself. She'd deal with that dragon later. It wasn't a very big dragon compared to those that had been faced and fought. Not a very big dragon with Cody's love wrapped around her in warmth and ecstasy.

But it was there, it existed. Its name was loss and it haunted her.

"Don't leave me," Cody said suddenly.

"I won't," she whispered.

"You did. For a minute you did." He turned her chin up, gazing deeply into her eyes. "You weren't there."

Brooke smiled at him slowly. "I love you."

Cody looked into her eyes, those eyes that were

greener than any green he'd ever seen, and the touch of coldness left him. He kissed her tenderly, held her close as sleep crept over them.

And he dreamed of fighting a dragon in the dark.

Eight

It was the sun that woke her, the sun and a niggling sensation of something being different, something being strange. She kept her eyes closed for a moment, trying to figure out what it was.

What was it?

Then she remembered; it all came back to her in a warm rush of memory. Her eyes opened slowly, and she turned her head to gaze at the face so close to her own. He was lying on his stomach beside her, his arm securely across her middle, and the sunlight striking across his face made him truly the golden man of her imagery.

Brooke looked at him as if she'd never seen him before, studied the classical planes and angles of his face with the total absorption of a brand-new lover. In the sane light of day she could hardly believe the turbulent emotions of last night; at the same time she didn't doubt them. Her love for Cody welled up inside her, threatening to spill over, filling all the places in her that had been dark and empty before he came.

As she watched him Cody stirred slightly and tightened his arm across her, smiling. "Brooke," he murmured in a satisfied tone without opening his eyes.

"At least you remember who I am," she said solemnly.

"First rule in the book of gentlemanly manners," he told her, golden eyes opening and glowing brightly at her. "Always remember in the morning whom you took to bed with you the night before."

"Oh, is *that* all?" she mourned. "I thought I might have stood out in your mind for some reason."

He chuckled softly, raising up on an elbow and gazing down at her. "You do, love. You certainly do," he murmured. And proved it.

When Brooke got her breath back, she discovered that her arms were around his neck. "Good morning," she said huskily.

"Good morning, darling." He was smiling.

She reached to push back a lock of golden hair falling over his forehead, feeling a sudden surge of possessiveness that surprised her. Twentieth-century woman or not, liberated or not, independent or not, a cavewoman deep inside of her thrilled to the certainty of touching her man.

"You have a very odd look in your eyes," Cody observed, watching her.

Brooke pushed the surprising thoughts aside and smiled up at him. "What would you like for breakfast?" she asked

"You," he answered promptly.

"Great minds . . ." Her smile slowly widened. "I was thinking along those lines myself. . . ."

It was Cody who first noticed, sometime later, that nature seemed to have gotten over her stormy mood. The early-morning sun didn't duck behind lowering clouds by lunchtime, as it had for weeks, but continued to shine brightly in a sky that shocked with its blueness. And, though neither Cody nor Brooke regretted the weather that had kept them indoors all this time, both were ready for fresh air and sunshine.

There was a foot of snow covered with a thick layer of ice and several more inches of snow on top of that outside, along with drifts of snow up to several feet that could easily catch the unwary by surprise. But the sunshine made of it a glittering white wonderland, and it beckoned to them.

So they bundled up for warmth and, accompanied by Phantom, went out to brave the unexpected drifts. It was Cody's first real chance to see the lodge and surrounding property in the clear light of day, and the sheer vastness of it surprised him.

"Is that a pasture?" he asked once, pointing to a line of fence barely visible on the other side of the valley.

"Uh-huh. It's empty at the moment; a horse breeder a few miles from here leases it every summer for his stock."

"How many acres?" Cody asked again absentmindedly as he cleared snow away from the barn door.

"Three hundred. Most of that small mountain, in fact."

Cody leaned on his shovel and stared at the "small" mountain. To his Texas-bred eyes anything taller than a molehill was huge; that mountain looked like Olympus. "You own that mountain?" he asked carefully.

Brooke was kneeling in the snow massaging Phantom's leg, they'd removed the splint this morning. She glanced over at Cody with a tiny smile. "Well, actually," she murmured, "I own—uh—all the land you can see from here."

Cody stared at her. Then he turned his gaze to all the land he could see. Counting the "small" mountain, there were four of them flanking the valley, and the valley itself must have covered nearly a hundred acres. He looked back at Brooke and said solemnly, "Marry me."

"That wasn't a very flattering proposal," she reproved. "I feel like part of a package deal."

"So sorry."

"Mmm." She lifted an eyebrow at his grin, then added conversationally, "You'd better not stand in front of the door when you lift the catch."

Cody, who'd set his shovel aside and started to open the door, received the advice just a moment too late. He managed to avoid the door shooting outward by stepping hastily aside, but one of Mister's rear hooves landed neatly on his instep as the burro charged out of the barn.

"Ouch!" Cody sat down rather hard in the snow, holding his foot and glaring at the faded gray burro that had halted a few feet away from the barn. Mister glared right back at him.

Brooke was maintaining a straight face through sheer effort. "I warned you," she reminded with a saintly air.

Cody struggled to his feet, obviously unhurt, and gave her a look of mock appreciation. "So you did. Remind me to thank you for that."

"I don't think I will," Brooke said warily.

"Smart lady."

Mister discovered an additional enemy just then, braying raucously as his bleary gaze focused on

Phantom. The burro lowered his head as if he were a bull getting ready to charge, an action that the wolf viewed with daunting disinterest and that made Brooke rise hastily to her feet.

"Oh, no, you don't!" she warned the burro, stepping between them. "I'll put you back in your stall, you bad-tempered animal, and not let you out until spring! Mind your manners—if you have any!"

The fact that Mister raised his head and proceeded to ignore the wolf was, of course, entirely unconnected with her warning. He proved that rather pointedly by feigning interest in Cody's shovel and then by trying to take a bite out of Cody's jacket.

Preserving his jacket with a neat sidestep, Cody kept a wary eye on the burro and addressed Brooke. "How old did you say he was?"

"Around thirty, I think. He moves pretty good for an old man, doesn't he?"

"He's part rattlesnake; you can see it in his eyes."

"I told you he hated every living thing."

"Would he really bite me?"

"If you gave him half a chance."

Cody sighed. "Knocked in the snow by a woman and then a burro; I must be losing my touch."

"Would you stop reminding me about that!"

"I was hoping you'd feel sorry for me," he apologized gravely.

"Why for heaven's sake?"

"So you'll marry me, of course."

"I'd never marry a man because I felt sorry for him."

"Then I'll have to try something else," he said thoughtfully.

No mention of marriage had been made until these two light references, and Brooke passed them off as casually as possible. She realized that beneath the banter Cody was entirely serious, but she wasn't yet ready to commit herself. The last dragon still remained to be faced and fought, the barrier of her fear defeated, and she wasn't sure how to do that.

But in the meantime Cody's lighthearted manner, his loving, teasing presence, went far in showing her what love was all about.

"Help!"

Brooke leaned against the barn and watched, totally deadpan, as Cody trampled a neat path around the barn. At her feet sat Phantom, and both observed the little game with detached interest. On his third circuit, Brooke helpfully noted that Mister was an old burro and probably wouldn't be able to chase him around a fourth time.

But the burro, taking advantage of the beaten path, seemed to be gaining a bit on his quarry by the fourth go-round.

As Cody panted around the corner Brooke pointed out, "He wouldn't chase you if you'd stop running." She was trying desperately not to laugh, well aware that Cody was running because he was enjoying the game.

"There's an old proverb," Cody gasped as he passed her. " 'Better to say he ran here, and not he died here.' " He disappeared around the other corner with Mister almost literally breathing down his neck.

Giggling, Brooke listened as a sudden curse tinted the cold air blue. Then she heard Mister bray triumphantly and watched as the burro came barreling back around the same corner, Cody's wool cap in his mouth. A hatless Cody was in hot pursuit.

"You moth-eaten donkey!" he roared wrathfully. "Come back here with my hat!"

Brooke burst out laughing.

"I'm going to have that animal stuffed."

"Cody—"

"I'll tie branches to his head and with any luck a hunter'll mistake him for a deer and shoot him."

"Cody—"

"Sic 'im, Phantom!"

"Just because he stole your hat—"

"And buried it!"

"I—uh—meant to warn you about this habit he has of hiding things. He's worse than a crow."

"My darling love, d'you see a pained expression upon my face?"

"Uh . . . yes."

"D'you detect a certain gleam in my eyes?"

"Now that you mention it—"

"Observe my hands reaching for you."

"Cody? Cody, you wouldn't— Cody? Help! Phantom, help!"

"That looks like a comfortable snowbank—"

"*Cody!*"

Days passed, days of beautiful weather and laughter and love. They played in the snow like children during the days, drawing even closer to each other through laughter. And at night they drew closer as man and woman, exploring the depth and meaning of their love.

They shared the daily chores of cooking and cleaning and getting wood for the fire. They argued spiritedly about the best way to renovate the old sled they had discovered in the barn, then took turns being buried in snowdrifts because neither one could steer the thing. They took long walks with Phantom, both to exercise his injured leg and to explore their surroundings. They found an old harness in the barn loft and managed to put it on an indignant Mister, trying for three days to persuade the old burro to pull a large piece of tin across the snow with them aboard.

They built a snowman. Then a snow castle. Then made unartistic stabs at snow images of Phantom and Mister. They got gloriously tipsy on Cody's eggnog recipe and held a solemn conversation on the merits of eggnog to cure all ills. They called Maine to check on the progress of Thor, Pepper, and babies, discovering that Thor was still somewhat incoherent, Pepper blissful, and twins doing nicely, thank you very much.

They made love.

They were never bored with each other, never restless. There was always something to do or say—or both. Always the feeling that it was new, that *they* were new and fascinating. The world might have stopped and left them to themselves

"You remind me of Venus."

"Oh? How's that?"

" 'Venus thy eternal sway, all the race of men obey' —or something like that."

"I thought you meant the planet."

"Funny."

"Well, how was I to know? You're always comparing me to one odd thing or another."

"I resent that."

"*You* resent it?"

"I've never compared you to anything odd."

"Oh, yeah?"

"Yeah."

"You compared me to Queen Victoria yesterday just because I said 'We are not amused' when you put that hat on Mister."

"She may or may not have been an odd thing: the point's debatable."

"And you compared me to a Pekingese when I put my hair up last night."

"They're cute—not odd."

"And Van Gogh after my portrait of Phantom in the snow."

"He was a very great man."

"And then—"

Silence.

"Uh . . . what was that for?"

"I had to shut you up somehow."

"I'll talk more often. . . ."

"You won't be able to do it."

"My darling love. Watch me."

"Cody, you won't be able to."

"Remember the bit about impossible things."

"Believing six of them before breakfast? Are we wandering through Alice's mirror?"

"Exactly. Want to attend the Mad Hatter's tea party?"

"Before or after I bury you?"

"You think he'll kill me, huh?"

"I wouldn't waste my money betting against the possibility."

"Such faith you have in me!"

"It's experience with Mister that I have."

"Hey! I grew up on a ranch, remember."

"Well, Mister didn't."

"So?"

"No respect for cowboys."

"I'll teach him."

"I doubt it."

"It just takes a bit of timing and— There! Hi-yo, Silver!"

Crunch.

"My darling love—"

"Uh-huh?"

"Want to stop giggling long enough to help me out of this snowbank?"

"I thought I'd go to a tea party. . . ."

"The woman thinks she's a comedian."

"The man thinks he's John Wayne."

"The man thinks he's freezing his—"

"Language!"

". . . ego off."

"I'm contemplating a new artistic creation."

"What's that?"

"*Cody in the Snow.* Thor would enjoy it, I think."

"Did you read that story called 'He Killed the Woman He Loved'?"

"Must have missed that one."

"Just let me get out of this damn snowbank . . ."

"Such beauty. Such ravishing beauty!"

"Then three cups of flour, and—"

"Helen of Troy."

"Mix it with—"

"Athena."

"You forgot the eggs."

"No, I didn't. Venus."

"Stop licking the spoon; I haven't finished with it yet."

"Couldn't resist. Mona Lisa."

"Are we having the same conversation here?"

"I don't think so."

"What're you talking about?"

"You. In comparison to other beautiful things."

"I see."

"What about you?"

"Can't you tell? I'm trying to fix this cake you wanted."

"Ah."

"So make up your mind."

"Hmm?"

"Whether you want the cake or my neck."

"Can't I have both?"

"Not at the same time. Either the cake or myself will fall."

"Hard decision."

"Flip a coin."

"Heads, it's you; tails, it's the cake."

"Well?"

"Heads."

"Let me see— Cody, that's a two-headed coin!"

"No kidding."

"You're a devious man."

"But you love me?"

"But I love you."

"Did you see that? A shooting star."

"Make a wish," Cody told her.

Brooke closed her eyes and wished, enfolded in the warmth of his embrace as they stood just outside the back door and waited for Phantom.

"What did you wish for?" he asked presently.

She was silent for a moment, once again looking up at the stars shining in a clear night sky. "I wished . . . for impossible things. D'you believe in impossible things, Cody?"

"I always have," he murmured.

There was a mournful, eerie howl, and both of them watched as Phantom stood in the snow-lightened darkness and stared off toward the mountains.

Softly Cody said, "I believe his mate will come

back, although, realistically, the odds are probably against it. I believe that moth-eaten burro will learn to love me one day. And I believe," he finished quietly, "that you'll defeat that last dragon, love."

She turned, staring up at him. "You knew—"

"That there was another one?" He smiled tenderly. "I knew. Impossible things, like dragons in the dark, and a beautiful woman with green eyes and ESP who loves me. A woman who's stronger than she knows, too strong to turn away from that last dragon. Too strong to let me help her fight it. Too strong to say she'll marry me with a dragon left to fight."

"I love you," she said unsteadily.

He pulled her close, held her tightly. "And I love you. Never forget that, my Brooke. Never forget that I'll love you all the days of my life . . . and through all the eternities of whatever comes after."

Shaken, she clung to him. "It's not a very big dragon," she promised in a whisper. "It doesn't breathe fire. But it's there. I—I have to deal with it."

"I know."

"And you *are* helping. By being you, you're helping."

"My love."

"Cody. . . ."

"What're you looking at?"

"You have a beauty mark beside your navel."

"That's what you're looking at?"

"It's shaped like a heart."

"Cody?"

"Hmm?"

"Look at me when I'm talking to you."

"I am looking at you."

"Look me in the eye, dammit."

"But it's so fascinating."

"My poor darling; you're losing your mind."

"*Darling.* It's just a word. Why does it sound so different when you say it?"

"What does it sound like?"

"Moonlight. Magic."

"Impossible things?"

"Impossible things. . . ."

The passing days were too full for Brooke to spend time brooding, but sometimes she woke in the night, Cody's arms holding her warmly, and wondered at the stubborn fear shaped like a gossamer dragon.

Loss.

She'd lost her father. Her mother in a different way. Josh. And it was reasonable, she knew, to fear loss. With life so uncertain, people dealt with a fear of loss every day. They loved in spite of the fear, had families in spite of the fear.

What made her fear different?

Sheltered in the haven of his arms, she fought to untangle confused strands of thought. She loved Cody; no matter what happened, nothing would ever change that. She knew that he loved her. He made her laugh and moved her almost unbearably, and showed her in a thousand different ways that she was special and that he loved her.

He had forced her to face the dragons she'd locked away inside of her for years, guided her gently and patiently through the maze of memory and bitterness. He had helped her to focus on the core of bitterness, lancing the painful wound to allow the poison to seep away.

He had softened and blurred the years of facing

crowds of strangers, understanding her psychic abilities without the undue emphasis that had always made her wary of "believers" encountered in her life.

To Cody, she realized, her ESP was simply another facet of her personality, of herself. Brooke had green eyes, black hair, and ESP. He accepted it calmly, cheerfully—lovingly. He loved her, not *despite* her ESP, and not *because* of it. He simply loved her.

Light shone in a dark corner of her mind, and Brooke fumbled for understanding of it.

Was part of her fear of losing Cody tangled up with the memories etched in her mind, memories of others who'd understood—for a while? Others who had expressed some degree of understanding—only to step back hurriedly when she had absently and accidentally looked into their minds? Did the hurt child inside of her fear the day when Cody would step back as well, when he'd look at her with that uneasy, mistrustful expression in his golden eyes?

Was that a part of it?

She thought about it, exploring her own mind with the probing touch he had taught her. And she realized that it was a part of the fear. At the same time she also realized that it was built out of bitter memories holding little power over her now, built on the blanket memory of many rather than on the certain knowledge of him.

Cody would never do that, Brooke told herself.

Because he was Cody. The sensitivity and understanding within him wasn't merely lip service; it was innate to him, and it went deeper than she would have believed possible. Of his own volition, he'd stripped himself bare for her, showed her the parts of himself that people usually guarded so jealously. Cody erected no barriers between them, built no walls. Even the normal, wary guarding of his innermost self was absent with her.

Because he loved her.

And was Brooke the child still crying in a dark room because perhaps there were monsters in the corner? The child who was too afraid to get up and turn on a light?

She faced the fear of loss with her certain knowledge of Cody, her understanding, finally, that the past held no terrors for her now. Cody would never back away from her as others had done. His Brooke had green eyes, black hair, and ESP, and he loved her.

The gossamer dragon faded almost to nothing, its transparency so fragile and unthreatening that even a sigh could defeat it. And Brooke sighed softly, raggedly, as the dragon vanished like a soap bubble.

Cody, she realized, was the light the child needed to reveal those dark corners. He was the warmth and security that gave her the courage to look and see what was there. And the man's love gave strength to the woman—strength and humor and the clarity of vision to see herself as he saw her.

The past fell away from her then, fully and completely. It broke away from her in shards made up of fears and hurts and years of loneliness, leaving behind a whole human being with scars healing in the light of understanding and love.

She was Brooke Kennedy. She knew karate, and how to drive a Sno-Cat. She could cook and knit, and loved murder mysteries. She played chess. She was well-educated because of brilliant tutoring and her own love of reading. She wasn't afraid of people. She wasn't burdened with a curse. She had black hair, green eyes, and ESP. And she loved Cody Nash.

"Brooke?"

It was a sleepy inquiry, his arm drawing her closer, and Brooke smiled into the darkness.

"Nothing, darling. Go back to sleep."

"Mmm. Love you," he murmured.

Still smiling, Brooke snuggled close to him. "I love you too, darling," she whispered. And drifted off to sleep.

Nine

"Well?" the dragon demanded somewhat sternly. "Have you stopped crying about imagined monsters in dark corners?"

Brooke sat at the bow, looking absently down into the black pit. She raised her eyes finally, gazing at the feathered, familiar, increasingly dear dragon of her dreamworld. "I have to risk it," she said slowly. "I have to risk—whatever might be there."

"Why?" he proded.

"Because—because even if there are monsters, even if I lose . . . I'll never lose what Cody's given me. And because he's the light I need to see into those dark corners."

The dragon applauded softly, his long-clawed dragon hands comical in the human gesture. "I thought you'd never figure it out," he confided dryly.

She was surprised. "It's that simple?"

"It always was. But that crying child had to stop crying long enough to see it. She'd hidden away in the dark for so long that it didn't seem possible to her that there was any way to deal with the darkness. Now she knows differently."

Brooke smiled. "Then I won't be afraid anymore?"

"Well, I wouldn't go that far just yet. You have to learn to pay no attention to those dark corners. And you have to learn to give of yourself totally; you haven't learned that yet. But your man is patient. He'll wait until you finally turn him into a prince."

"I haven't done that yet?"

"No."

Puzzled, Brooke asked, "How will I do that?"

The dragon smiled oddly. "How soon we forget. With a kiss, of course."

"I've kissed Cody!"

With a chuckle the dragon murmured, "Not like that, you haven't."

"But, how—"

"You'll know the difference." And without another word the dragon vanished.

Brooke woke up abruptly, confused for a moment because the dream had ended so suddenly. Cautiously she raised up on an elbow, gazing at the peacefully sleeping face of the man she loved. He was lying close beside her on his stomach, his arm across her middle.

She thought of the dream. It was easy to understand the part about learning to ignore dark corners, but—open up totally? Turn him into her prince? What was her mind trying to tell her?

She watched the sunlight crawl across his face, waiting for the slight stirring as he fought his way up from sleep. And before he could open his eyes, she said solemnly, "I love you, Cody Nash."

His golden eyes opened, blurred from sleep for a moment and then clearing, brightening. He rolled over and pulled her on top of him in one smooth motion, smiling up at her. "Such a nice way to wake up," he murmured, kissing her. "And I love you, too, ma'am."

"Isn't it nice?" she asked happily.

"Masterly understatement." Cody grinned. " 'Nice' doesn't begin to describe it, darling."

"Inadaquate words," she said, her lips thoughtfully exploring the angle of his jaw. "We're hampered by them."

"How about actions?" he suggested.

"Actions are nice. I approve of actions."

"Your wish is my command, darling love. . . ."

"You tried this before, love," she reminded.

"There's a knack to it. And I think I've got it now."

"Maybe you'd better give me your parents' address first."

"Funny."

"What kind of flowers d'you want on the wreath?"

"You're undermining my confidence here!"

"It's just that I really prefer you with unbroken bones."

"I have to hold his head up, that's all."

"I can't talk you out of it, huh?"

"I *refuse* to admit defeat."

"Stand back, Phantom."

"Now. Just hang on with the knees, and—"
Crunch.

"Darling Brooke."

"Yes, love?"

"John Wayne bit the dust. Or snow, as the case happens to be."

"I noticed."

"Want to lend a hand?"

"If I leave you there, maybe you'll stop trying to master the donkey."

"That animal's laughing at me."

"I wasn't talking about Mister."

"Oh, funny."

Cody never did get Mister to accept a passenger.

Several days passed. Cody, being a free-lance troubleshooter, didn't worry overmuch that his vacation had lasted longer than he'd planned. And Brooke was content to have this time to explore her awakened emotions.

So they spent the days outside in the sunshine loving and the nights inside the house loving.

And then, late one afternoon while they were having a cheerful, exuberant snow fight near the back porch, Brooke's last dragon forced its way out. It was only a shadow of what it had been, but its time had come and its presence had to be acknowledged out loud.

Brooke was laughing, but suddenly her laughter was cut off and she turned her head sharply, away from the lodge and Cody.

He stepped toward her, watching her intently. "What is it?"

Her reply was little more than a whisper, a breath of sound. "Look."

Cody followed her gaze, focusing on the clump of trees nearly sixty feet from the lodge, where Phantom had first appeared. For a moment he saw nothing. But a distant motion far to the right caught his attention, and he looked up toward the ridge high above the valley. Three, four, five. Five indistinct gray shapes against the backdrop of snow. Wolves. And they stood still and silent, looking down on the humans below.

Shifting his gaze back to the clump of trees, Cody immediately saw what Brooke had sensed.

The she-wolf they'd named Psyche was coal-black from nose to tail and nearly as large as Phantom. She emerged from the trees warily, watching the two humans with the inborn caution of a wild thing. Her tail was held low, her ears up alertly; she was thin but not overly so, and her thick coat gleamed with health.

She halted a few feet out of the trees, the coating of ice over two feet of snow supporting her weight easily. She didn't howl, but as her yellow eyes located Phantom lying on the back porch, a peculiar puppylike yipping sound came from her throat.

Brooke and Cody half turned with one mind to look at Phantom, watching as he rose unhurriedly to his feet and came toward them; they were standing between him and Psyche. He hardly limped now, his injured leg healed from their care, and he was sleek and healthy. He halted between the two humans, looking up at each of them in turn.

Brooke reached out to scratch gently between the pointed ears. "You come back to see us, Phantom," she told him huskily, and Cody added a soft "Anytime" as he, too, touched the wolf.

His tail waved once, and then Phantom was trotting confidently across the space separating him and his mate. She welcomed him with a curious dignity mixed with coquettishness. Noses touched, a black tail and a gray one waved happily. More of the soft yipping sounds came from her throat and his. And then they turned together toward the woods.

Phantom looked back once, a brief hesitation that might have been a good-bye and perhaps a thank you. And then they vanished into the trees.

Brooke found that she was reaching for Cody's hand even as he reached for hers. They stood silently, their eyes turned up toward the ridge and the other waiting wolves. In time the gray and black leaders joined the rest of the pack, and there was a blur of excited motion as Phantom was welcomed back.

As the others vanished along the ridge a lone wolf remained to gaze down on the valley. Motionless, he might have been carved from granite—or from dream. He stood for a long moment until his black mate joined him to stand by his side. Then they turned away, drifting along the ridge side by side until they were lost from sight.

"She came back," Brooke murmured. She turned glowing eyes up to Cody. "She came back for him."

Smiling, Cody drew her into his arms. "And they lived happily ever after," he said softly.

"They would," Brooke said slowly, "if this were a fairy tale. But it isn't. There are traps, ranchers with stock to protect, hunters. Nature's own savagery. Man encroaching on their hunting grounds."

"But they'll live," Cody reminded.

"For how long?" Brooke turned with him as they started into the house, her lovely face brooding over a fate that could strike down wolves—and men. "How long?"

Cody was silent while they removed and put away jackets and scarves, silent while they went into the den and sat on the couch before a cheerfully blazing fire.

He heard her question, and with his understanding of her he heard more than her words.

She'd lost so much, his Brooke. Her father, the love of a mother, her uncle. Her childhood, her privacy. He sensed that she had largely come to terms with what he now identified as the last dragon—largely, but not completely.

Brooke didn't want to lose anymore.

When Cody finally spoke, his voice was quiet and contemplative. He sat beside Brooke on the couch, his arm around her, and told her a story she had never heard.

"I knew a man once," he said slowly, "who had learned the hard way about reality. He watched his mother die by inches for years and saw his father killed before his eyes. And that man promised himself that no one would ever suffer because of him. He was convinced that he didn't have the right, that no one had the right, to cause others to suffer. He had a dangerous job, and though he lived with the danger, he refused to allow . . . others to live with the danger if he could prevent it."

Cody stared into the fire, his eyes far away. "So this man built a shell around himself. He was determined that if he were suddenly wiped out of existence, there would be nothing to cause anyone pain. He made acquaintances rather than friends and—shut out the friend of his childhood. Not because he felt too little, but because he felt too much.

"He wouldn't give hostages to fortune, or be a hostage himself. He wouldn't love because love caused pain, either by itself or through fear or loss. For the noblest of reasons he shut himself off from caring."

Brooke knew whom Cody was speaking of, although she'd never heard the story. "What happened?" she asked softly, knowing the result but not how it came about.

Cody smiled a little, still gazing into the fire. "He met a woman. And fate turned up a wild card in his deck. She knocked him right off all his preconceived ideas and left him totally bewildered. Because she was the exact opposite of him in one very important way. She embraced hostages. Wherever she went, she forged ties; whomever she met along the way was instantly a friend.

"And she was a gambler, this lady; that was what bewildered him. She knew that fate could roll the dice just once at any given moment and demand that she pay a price. But she loved in spite of that knowledge and understanding, loved cheerfully and happily. She'd seen harsh reality just as he had; she'd known loss and pain.

"But she charged into his life with the cheerful exuberance of a spring storm, bringing with her bits and pieces of life all over the world. She was truly 'a part of all she'd met' and like nothing else he'd ever known. And she loved him with a stubborn determination, demanding her right as a human being to love where she chose. He was her hostage, like it or not; he was the most vital hostage of all, and she was willing to risk.

"He couldn't stand against that, not even with the best of reasons or noblest of motives. Because he loved her too."

Cody fell silent, still looking into the fire.

"Thor," Brooke murmured. "And Pepper."

He nodded slightly. "Not too long ago, he and I were talking. It was one of those naked moments in life that come all too rarely even between close friends. He was talking about how Pepper had changed his life, his entire way of thinking. And there was . . . wonder in his voice. He said that it had taken him a long time to understand—to really understand. That the fear of losing what it had taken him so long to find had haunted him. But that he had slowly seen the truth, slowly understood what Pepper had known instinctively from the beginning."

"What was it?" Brooke asked quietly.

"That love doesn't weaken as it spreads." Cody spoke slowly, obviously reaching for words. "Doesn't lessen. And that those who love . . . boldly actually stand to lose less than those who hoard their love. Because the more you love, the less fate can hurt you. Loving freely and willingly isn't an invitation to loss; it's a protection against it."

Cody turned suddenly to gaze at her, his golden eyes very sure. "My darling love—don't you see? Love is as much a shield as a blanket; you carry it in your heart for warmth *and* protection. It isn't something you can ever lose, because it'll be with you all the days of your life."

Brooke fumbled for words. "But . . . *people* can be lost. They get—hit by buses and die in plane crashes and have heart attacks. And you can never be *sure* because there are no guarantees, no certainties. There are—possible monsters lurking around every corner. . . ."

"And happily-ever-after should be a promise? Is that what you want, my love? A guarantee?"

"I just can't bear to lose anymore," she whispered.

Cody lifted a hand to touch her cheek softly. "In the fairy tales happily-ever-after ends the story," he reminded gently. "There is no more. No highs or lows. No loose ends dangling." He smiled at her. "But in real life, happily-ever-after is just the beginning. It's where life starts. Oh, there might be monsters around this or that corner, but those monsters are kind of like your dragons, love. Once you face them and fight them, you usually discover that they weren't very fierce after all."

"And if they are?" She looked at him wistfully. "If they're too strong to fight and won't go away? If they—take something? Someone?"

"Then we go on," Cody said quietly. "Because we're meant to live, just like those wolves. And while we live, we do so the best way we can."

"My head understands that," Brooke told him. "But my heart— Cody, I know that I should be able to ignore those possible monsters. Why look for trouble? But I'm afraid. Not so afraid now as I was once; I know that I'll never lose what you've given me. I—I want you to understand that any reservations I have won't be because of you. I think that, like Thor, it's going to take me a while to fully understand."

She took a deep breath, only beginning to understand, only beginning to open up and give of herself completely. "There are parts of me no one's seen but you, and that doesn't frighten me anymore. I love you, Cody. And I'm willing to risk all the possible monsters lurking around corners."

His hands framed her face warmly, his golden eyes bright and full. "My darling love. Just as soon as we can dig our way out of this valley of yours, I'm taking you to church."

Brooke laughed shakily. "Was that a proposal?"

"That, my love, was a flat declaration of intent. I'm going to marry you, lady. In a double-ring ceremony with music and flowers. We can throw out the word *obey* if you like, but I want this union of ours tied up neatly with ribbons and binding wherever possible."

"Mmm." Brooke linked her fingers together at the back of his neck, smiling at him. "So masterful. Well, I suppose I'll have to go along with this caveman display—if only to save wear-and-tear on your ego."

"I'll get you for that."

"You certainly will."

"Cody?"

"Hmm?"

"What's your apartment like?"

"It needs a woman's touch," he said judiciously after a moment's thought.

Brooke snuggled a bit closer to him in the comfortable bed, giggling. "Now I know why you—uh—proposed."

"That's a slur on my character, woman."

"Probably the truth though."

"No such thing. I merely answered your question."

Suddenly serious she murmured, "I don't know . . . if I'll be able to cope with being around a lot of people again, darling."

He hugged her hard. "You'll cope, my love. We'll work it out so it won't be rough on you."

"How?" she asked wryly.

Cody chuckled. "Somehow. Not that I think you'll have any trouble. You're stronger than you know." He yawned hugely, adding comfortably, "We'll work something out."

Wonderingly she murmured, "Green eyes and ESP."

"Hmm?"

"It really doesn't bother you, does it?"

"What?"

"My peculiar abilities."

"*Which* peculiar abilities?"

"Very funny. The ESP."

"Oh. That."

"Yes—that!"

"My darling love," Cody said politely, "please remember that I've fought dragons for you. My magic sword may be a bit dented, but it remains intact. ESP is nothing."

"Really?"

"Really."

"I'm glad."

"Besides, it may come in handy."

"Ah? How?"

"We'll play bridge with Thor and Pepper, and won't even need signals."

She giggled. "That's cheating."

"So? Pepper cheats."

"At bridge?"

"At anything. The lady's ruthless."

"Didn't sound like she cheated in getting Thor."

"Yes, she did. I have it on the best authority that she openly and innocently declared her intentions of chasing him and, in so doing, knocked the poor guy completely off his guard."

"Oh? On whose authority?"

"Thor's."

Brooke giggled.

"Original approach, huh?" Cody observed thoughtfully.

"I'll say."

"And speaking of the new parents, I suppose we'd better call them tomorrow. Invite them to the wedding."

"Sounds good to me."

"Are we going to throw out *obey*?"

"Is that worrying you?"

"Not at all. I'm above such things."

"Uh-huh."

"I suppose we could leave it in. Traditional vows, and all that."

"Cody."

"Well, you need somebody to take care of you. And if you promise to obey, at least I've got a chance to do that."

"Noble reasoning?"

"Of course."

"Mmm. Well, I'll promise to obey within reason."

"I don't think that's the way it was written."

"I'm meeting you halfway on this; don't expect more."

"Uh . . . right. You'll love, honor, and obey within reason."

"It does sound strange when you put it like that."

"I hoped you'd notice."

"Nevertheless, I'm marrying you because I love you, not because I need a keeper."

"*Husband*," Cody told her, "originally meant 'caretaker.' "

"Are you sure about that?"

"Reasonably."

"I'll look it up tomorrow."

"D'you doubt my word?"

"Just your motives."

"That hurt."

"Sorry."

"And after all my patience too."

"That's what worries me."

"What?"

"Your patience. It's bound to have worn thin by now. For all I know you're ripe for revenge."

"Ha-ha."

"Well."

"My darling love, I solemnly promise never to take advantage of *your* promise to obey. How's that?"

"I'll think about it."

"Damn."

Brooke yawned. "We'll argue about it later."

"I never argue," Cody protested, offended. "I reason."

"Then we'll *reason* later."

"Yes, ma'am."

"Cody?"

"Hmm?"

"Can we have a cat?"

"We'll have a panther if you like."

"The indulgent husband."

"Always."

"I suppose I should make the best deal I can now, while you're still the happy bridegroom-to-be?"

"Your chances for stacking the deck in your favor will never be better."

"I'll make up a list of demands."

"You do that."

"Will they be honored?"

"Within reason."

"I knew you wouldn't be able to resist that."

"Say good night, my love. We have a big day ahead of us tomorrow."

"How so?"

"Tomorrow we start digging out."

"So soon?"

"You betcha. We're heading for the altar, *obey* or no *obey*."

"My darling Cody—if it means so much to you, I'll promise to obey. I'd hate for you to ruin your track record by losing patience with me."

"I'd *never*—"

"Good night, darling."

"Pepper? Pepper!" Cody shook his head slightly

and shot Brooke a laugh-filled grin. "She's dropped the phone. I heard a panicked yell from Thor just a minute before. D'you suppose he'll ever get the hang of being a father?"

Brooke started laughing. "I don't know, but Pepper may have to hire a nurse for the babies and spend her time soothing her husband!"

"Pepper? Oh—you're back. What happened?"

He listened for a moment, his grin widening, then lifted an eyebrow at Brooke. "One of the twins got the hiccups."

"And Thor panicked?"

Cody listened a bit longer, then burst out laughing. To Brooke he explained, "Pepper says he's throwing back straight whiskey and muttering something about hostages."

"Poor man."

"Listen, Pepper, we just— Right. A couple of weeks probably. Now, don't start arranging a— Pepper? Pepper!"

He hung up the phone and turned to Brooke, shaking his head. "She hung up. Her excuse was feeding time, but I know her. The woman's ruthless. She's probably on the phone now booking Saint Peter's Cathedral for the wedding."

"Was she surprised?" Brooke had spoken only briefly to Pepper, allowing Cody to break the news.

"No," he said wryly. He pulled her to her feet, wrapping his arms around her. "My darling love, Pepper had this planned from the beginning. I suspected as much when I came up here, but once I'd met you, I didn't give a damn whose the original idea was."

"Mmm." Brooke reached up suddenly, pulling his head down and kissing him very tenderly.

Cody smiled at her. "Well, what'd I do to deserve that?"

"Oh . . . nothing." Brooke smiled slowly. "I just decided it was time to turn my dragon into my prince."

"My Brooke . . ."

"Cody? Uh . . . I thought we were going to start digging out?"

"Later."

Ten

"You know," Cody said musingly, "I think Thor's finally gotten the hang of being a daddy."

They were driving south along the Maine coastline, heading for their apartment-home in Virginia. It was a fairly long trip by car, but both Brooke and Cody enjoyed the drive; they had made it several times during the past two years.

Sitting close beside her husband in the powerfully purring Mercedes, Brooke laughed. "You noticed that, too? I think I realized it when Jenna fell down and skinned her knee, and instead of calling an ambulance, Thor just put a Band-Aid on it and told her to watch where she was going."

Cody chuckled softly. "Quite a change, isn't it? But he's had two years with the twins; it's high time he realized that they aren't made of glass. One hour with the indestructible Master Jamie should prove that to anyone; I fished him out of the lake twice and rescued two ducks and one frog from his inquisitive little fingers. Thor threatened to put a leash on him."

"You men came up with the idea of the picnic," Brooke reminded dryly. "And if you hadn't mentioned the lake, Jamie wouldn't have demanded to see the ducks."

"Mmm." After a moment Cody said with deceptive casualness, "Pepper was certainly glowing."

"She always does," Brooke murmured offhandedly.

Cody looked at his wife, opened his mouth to say something, then apparently thought better of it. Brooke watched him for a while, smiling, then relented.

"Yes," she said, as if Cody had asked a question.

He grinned. "Really? Thor doesn't know yet, I take it?"

"No. Pepper just found out; the doctor called with the test results while we were packing the picnic basket, as a matter of fact. She's planning to tell him tonight."

"Wonder how he'll take it this time," Cody mused.

"I don't know, but I'd love to be a fly on the wall."

"How does Pepper think he'll take it?"

Brooke giggled suddenly. "Well, she told me quite cheerfully that he'd go off the deep end, especially since it'll be a cesarean delivery. Apparently that was what nearly flattened him when the twins were born; Pepper hadn't warned him because she didn't want him to worry."

"Poor Thor," Cody murmured.

"He'll survive." Brooke told her husband, resting her head on his shoulder with a smile. Now? she wondered, then decided not. He was driving a car, after all. She was reasonably sure that Cody would be delighted by her news and not go off the deep end. Reasonably sure. They both wanted children, although they'd been in no hurry about it.

Still, she had a suspicion that Cody, amused though he was by his friend Thor's bemused fatherhood, would be a bit less casual about his own offspring. He probably wouldn't go into a tail-spin over each tear from an infant eye, but she considered it an ironclad certainty that any child of theirs would have to be guarded against being spoiled to death by his or her father.

The soft music playing on the car's radio was the only sound to break the silence between them—a companionable silence. Dreamily Brooke allowed her mind to wander back over the two years of happiness that had more than made up for the pain and bitterness that had gone before.

They had kept the lodge in Montana, dividing the year fairly equally between it and the apartment in Virginia. It might, perhaps, have seemed curious to some people that Brooke and Cody could enjoy going off to spend as much as six months at a time way out in the back of beyond with only each other for company; it didn't seem so to them.

Cody had decided to stop traveling, becoming instead a free-lance consultant with a partner and a fixed office in Washington, D.C. And that, too, probably seemed curious to outsiders, because his partner in the business was, like Cody, a man who preferred to work only several months a year. So the two men divided equal time at the office, giving each as much as six months away from it.

It had worked out beautifully for Brooke and Cody. She enjoyed the contact with other people she met through Cody's work, now finding herself relaxed and casual even around strangers. And the time spent together at the lodge had strengthened the bond between her and Cody, giving them the chance to know each other with a thoroughness rarely possible for other couples in the hectic pace of modern life.

They'd been so lucky, she thought, to find each other. And lucky to have been snowed in at the lodge all during those first weeks because it had drawn them closer and given them the time they'd needed to find each other.

So lucky . . .

Cody realized that she'd fallen asleep, her head resting familiarly on his shoulder. He shifted position only slightly, drawing her a bit closer and making sure that she was comfortable. They'd had to start for home early this morning because he had a business appointment tomorrow, and he wondered anxiously if the poker game last night, lasting well into the morning hours because he and Thor had been struggling against Brooke's ESP and Pepper's clear cheating, had tired her too much.

He delighted in pampering her, in taking care of her. Brooke was a strong woman; he didn't often get the chance to baby her openly. There had been a bout with the flu last winter; she'd laughed at him for his anxious concern, but he could remember her bemused surprise at being taken care of by him.

That she could still be surprised by that told Cody her scars were still present, and he wanted to wrap her in his love until the warmth of it wiped out the past.

As for himself, Cody, too, felt surprise. Whenever his gaze fell on her, whenever her green eyes met his, whenever she touched him, he felt the delighted surprise that she loved him. That feeling had never dimmed, never lessened. It was something he never wanted to lose. When they were old and gray, he knew instinctively that he would still look at her with surprise, the surprise of a man who'd stumbled on a pearl far, far beyond price and been given the inestimable right of calling it his.

God, how he loved her!

Sunning himself in the bright warmth of that feeling, Cody rubbed his chin gently against his sleeping wife's forehead, heading for home.

Brooke enjoyed her dream visits with the dragon, even though she was aware that it was just her own mind finding a way to solve problems and hold discussions with itself. The dreams were by no means every-night occurrences; in two years worth of nights, she could count the dreams on her fingers.

So they were rare enough still to hold enchantment, and she looked forward to them. But it seemed that she'd outgrown her need for the dragon's counsel; he told her so himself.

"Ah, you've come to say good-bye," he told her in a pleased voice, his undragonlike features brightening.

"Good-bye?" Brooke sat in the bow of her little boat and stared at him. "I don't want to say good-bye!"

"You didn't want to jump into the pit either," he reminded.

"I was afraid then! I'm not afraid anymore."

"That's why you no longer need me," he said gently.

Brooke stared at him and felt a sudden sadness, an abrupt sense of something that felt like loss.

"You haven't lost me," the dragon told her, floating nearer. "I'll always be a part of you. And that's the difference now."

"I don't understand," she murmured.

"Yes, you do." He smiled. "You came to me that first time divided. The child in you had just awakened and the woman was confused by that. So I had to show you both sides of yourself."

The bright golden eyes laughed at her. "You see—you do understand!"

"Yes." She looked at him. "But I'll miss you."

Chuckling, the dragon floated back a bit and held out his arms. "Enough of that. Jump one last time."

Brooke stood up, balancing easily in the bow. "Will you catch me this time?" she asked.

"This time," he promised, smiling.

She jumped and he caught her, his body warm and hard and familiar. And the pit was warm darkness and the sound of a heart beating. . . .

Brooke woke with a start, remembering immediately where she was. She blinked and raised her head from Cody's shoulder, smothering a yawn with one hand.

"Ready for lunch?" He was smiling down at her. "Or do you need the sleep more than food?"

She felt her stomach rumble and laughed. "Food, definitely." Surprised, she saw that the Mercedes was pulling into the parking lot of the seafood restaurant that was a favorite of theirs on this trip. "Here already? Heavens, how long have I been sleeping?"

"Hours," Cody responded politely. "And very boring it's been for me, let me tell you!"

"Sorry, love," Brooke murmured, kissing his chin. The kiss nearly cost both the Mercedes and a red Cougar their bumpers, since Cody was a bit distracted while maneuvering into a parking space.

"You almost caused me to bob that Cougar's tail," Cody told her severely as they got out of the Mercedes.

Brooke smiled at him, and then hastly smothered another yawn. "It wouldn't have done the Mercedes much good either," she noted.

He caught her hand as they started up the walk, looking concerned. "No more late nights for you, wife. You're looking a little pale, and you obviously didn't get enough sleep even with the nap."

"I'm fine," Brooke promised lightly, preceding him into the restaurant.

If the timing hadn't been wrong again, she would have explained that both the slight pallor and her sleepiness were merely symptoms. And those symptoms had prompted Pepper to suggest to Brooke that she ought to visit a doctor and get it confirmed.

Once over the shock, Brooke had laughed at her own blindness; she'd honestly thought she was coming down with something like the flu, and had avoided telling Cody about the afternoon naps she'd been taking. Sleepiness and pallor aside, though, she felt wonderful. And whether it was her own consciousness of eating for two or nature's prodding, her appetite satisfied even Cody's watchful gaze.

Once back on the road again, they whiled away the time and the miles with easy conversation.

It was late when they reached their apartment outside D.C., and as Cody unlocked and opened the door a twenty-pound bundle of odd-colored fur launched itself at them from the entrance hall table. Cody caught the cat with an expertise born of practice, shooting Brooke an amused look.

"I think he missed us."

"I'd say so. Hello, Falstaff."

Falstaff blinked china-blue eyes happily at her. He was unusual in the feline kingdom, being unfettered by reserve, independence, arrogance, or any other catlike traits. A tongue-in-cheek gift from Pepper and Thor, Falstaff was the first offspring of their cat King Tut and the solid black Siamese mate Tut had brought home one day.

Unusual in his manners since Falstaff considered himself human, the cat was also unusual in appearance. He'd inherited most of his mother's coloring; he was solid black except for blond eyebrows and a peculiarly ringed blond-and-black tail. But he'd inherited the Siamese eyes and voice from his father, and he used the latter to complain raucously as he was set on the floor about being abandoned for the better part of three days.

Reading a note that had been left for them on the hall table, Brooke looked down at the nattering cat with a mock frown. "Stop complaining. Mrs. Peters not only fed you regularly, but she says that the two of you listened to music and sunned yourselves on the balcony yesterday." She sent an amused look toward her husband as he hung up their coats. "They also went for a drive; she spoils Falstaff to death."

Cody chuckled as he put an arm around his wife and led her down the hall. "Remember that her Siamese will be ready for a mate in a few months; I think she's contemplating a litter of interesting kittens."

"I bet she'll offer us pick of the litter," Brooke said.

"Fine with me," Cody responded equably. "Oh,

by the way, the Martins want us to come look at their pups. Are you sure you want a half-poodle half-Shetland sheepdog? Lord knows what he'll look like when he's grown."

"Adorable." Brooke laughed. "We'll need a bigger apartment."

"I was thinking we might start looking at houses," Cody said absently, rummaging through the refrigerator.

Brooke smiled to herself. "Sounds like a good idea to me."

"D'you think Phantom and Psyche will bring their pups to visit while we're at the lodge next summer?" Brooke asked casually. She glanced absently over at the corner of their bedroom, where Falstaff was reposing in his accustomed bed on a boudoir chair, and wondered briefly at a feline who could accept even wolves with complete calm. The cat was definitely uncatlike.

"Probably, since they did last summer," Cody responded as he came out of their bathroom. He regarded her sternly and changed the subject. "What have you done with my pajama bottoms, wench?"

Seated cross-legged on the bed brushing her long hair, Brooke lifted an eyebrow at him. "My dear husband, you haven't worn pajamas since the wedding night—and for some time before that, if I remember correctly."

"Ah. I knew something was missing."

"I didn't miss them."

He started laughing. "Well, if I can't wear pajamas, what're you doing in that thing?"

"That thing" was a baby-doll confection of black

satin and lace with about as much material as a lady's hankie.

"You bought it for me," Brooke reminded calmly. "And if I didn't have you to keep me warm, it'd never leave the dresser drawer; it's drafty as hell."

Laughing, Cody discarded his towel and sat down on the bed beside her. "It does wonders for my temperature!"

Brooke tossed her brush to the foot of the bed and leaned back on her pillow, smiling at him. Reading the gleam in his eyes, she decided that it was now or never. "Uh . . . Cody—"

"You're still pale," he discovered suddenly, frowning. "Honey, maybe you'd better see a doctor."

"Yes, well, I'm planning to make an appointment tomorrow."

"I *knew* there was something wrong! How do you feel?"

Brooke thought for a moment. "Different," she said judiciously. "Decidedly different."

Cody looked even more worried.

Hastily, Brooke said, "I probably shouldn't say anything, because I could be wrong, but somehow I don't think so. I—uh—I think we're expecting, Cody."

"Expecting what?" he said blankly.

Brooke laughed in spite of herself. "Now, look, love. You certainly don't need a lecture on how families grow!"

"Families? You mean—" His golden gaze dropped to his wife's flat stomach incredulously.

"That's it." She stared at him. "Cody? Snap out of it, love! Say something. Anything."

"A baby," he said. "Our baby."

Brooke watched his face with fascinated wonder. And she wished suddenly that she could film this moment and his face, just to be able to show it, in the distant future, to a child not yet born. *This is how your father looked when he knew you were on the way. This is how much he loved you even then. . . .*

"Cody . . ."

"Brooke . . . my Brooke." Golden eyes blazed down at her. Unsteadily he said, "I don't think—I'm going to be as calm about this—as I thought."

She smiled very tenderly. "I wouldn't have it any other way, love."

Epilogue

"Would I mind another what?" Thor asked absently, pulling a battered stuffed owl from under his pillow and staring at it. It was Jenna's owl, and he tossed back the covers with a sigh born of experience, knowing that if she woke up during the night and wasn't able to find Coco (odd name for a owl, he thought for the hundredth time), she'd have a two-year-old fit.

Sitting at the foot of the bed brushing her hair, Pepper hid a smile. "We'll talk about it when you get back," she murmured.

Thor went down the hall to the twins' bedroom, creeping in and hoping the dim night-light would show him the inevitable scattered toys before he broke his neck falling over one. He stepped over Fifi, the Doberman—the twins' self-appointed guardian—with an automatically soothing—if soft—murmur, and glanced in amusement at Brutus, the attack-trained Chihuahua, who was lying with his customary arrogance on the foot of Jamie's bed. Of King Tut there was no sign; temperamental Siamese and his black mate preferred to sleep downstairs on the couch.

Thor bent over the nearest small bed, very gently tucking Coco in the crook of a small arm.

Pausing for a moment, as he often did, he looked at his children and marveled silently.

He smiled slightly as he gazed down at the burnished red head on the pillow. She'd gotten his hair, little Jenna, and her mother's glorious violet eyes. And she'd be a delicate beauty one day; she could already wind anything not made of stone around her tiny finger.

Looking across to the other small bed, he saw the tumbled silver hair of Jamie, only that visible above the covers pulled up to his eyebrows. He'd already shot up taller than his sister, Thor reflected; the pediatrician had predicted an eventual six feet or more. Jamie, with the gray eyes of his father holding an expression uncannily like his mother's serene self-knowledge.

Thor shook his head slightly, bemusedly, wondering at these two tiny people that his and Pepper's love had created. Then he crept from the bedroom as silently as he'd come, cautiously avoiding two stuffed bears and an overturned dump truck.

When he returned to the master bedroom, it was to find his wife standing by the window, looking out over the darkened pasture below. Her silver hair shone as it hung down her back, contrasting beautifully with the black silk nightgown which clung lovingly to her slender body. Thor stood silently in the doorway for a moment, watching her because he loved to watch her without her awareness; it was in these unguarded moments that the depth of his love for her very nearly overwhelmed him.

His Pepper. At thirty-two she still carried the identification card that verified her age, and still had to show it occasionally. His beloved Pepper, the gambler and cardsharp; the matchmaker and mender of lonely hearts; the lover, the wife, the mother. Pepper, eternally mysterious, eternally fascinating even to the man who knew her so well. The woman who'd stolen his heart in spite of himself and taught him to love.

God, how he loved her. . . .

She turned away from the window, smiling across the room at him. "Kids still asleep?" she asked softly.

Thor went to her, held her in an embrace which still contained incredulity because she was his and he was almost afraid to believe it. "Can't you hear the silence?" he murmured huskily, kissing her.

Pepper linked her fingers together behind his neck. Smiling up at him, she said, "I asked you a question just before you went out."

"Mmm." He began nuzzling her throat. "I remember. You asked if I minded another something."

"Hostage," Pepper murmured dreamily. "Another hostage to fortune."

Thor lifted his head and stared at her. "I get the feeling, beloved," he said uneasily, "that you're not talking about the pony Jenna wants."

Pepper shook her head slowly.

"Then . . . you're . . . ?"

"Do I have to spell it this time?" she asked solemnly.

"Another hostage," Thor murmured dazedly. "Diapers and three o'clock feedings and colic."

"Sit down, darling."

"Picking the right name. Fastening your shoes because you can't reach them. Putting one of the cribs back together. Warming bottles."

"That's it. Now just lie back; it's time to go to bed, darling."

"Pepper," Thor said suddenly, clearly.

"Yes, darling?"

"The doctor said surgery. I distinctly remember—"

"He couldn't be sure, darling; it's not an ironclad rule these days that one cesarean has to follow another."

"Yes, but—he said you're so small—"

"Talking through his hat," Pepper murmured, climbing into bed beside her prostrate husband. Cheerfully she added, "Anyway, you and Cody can pace together; I have a feeling it'll be timed pretty closely."

"You mean they're . . .?"

"Think so."

A faintly gleeful expression stole into Thor's eyes. "That'll fix him. He thinks I don't know he's been laughing behind my back, but I do. I bet he'll stop laughing when he has to go through it himself!"

"I wouldn't be a bit surprised, darling," Pepper agreed gently. She cuddled up to her husband adoringly. "Not a bit surprised."

THE EDITOR'S CORNER

The holiday spirit is very much with all of us who work on LOVESWEPT . . . and, feeling like Santa's helpers, we're delighted to tell you about a few of the "surprise packages" you can expect from us next year.

In 1985 Bantam will publish long novels by four of your favorite LOVESWEPT authors. But these books won't be expanded LOVESWEPTS or, for that matter, books of any prescribed format or length. Indeed, the only thing they have in common is that they were written by LOVESWEPT authors! Each novel is different, the author's unique creation, and will be published in Bantam's general list without LOVESWEPT identification. (Never fear, though, that you'll miss these terrific books. I'll be giving you information and lots of reminders about their publication throughout the coming months.)

The first of the four fascinating works by LOVESWEPT authors that you can look forward to enjoying in 1985 is **SUNSET EMBRACE** by Sandra Brown. An ardent love story, a mesmerizing tale of past violence shadowing future happiness, **SUNSET EMBRACE** is a riveting historical set on a wagon train heading for Texas in 1872. A superb storyteller, Sandra has published her contemporary romances under the pen names of Erin St. Clair and Rachel Ryan; her one previous historical romance came out under the name Laura Jordan. **SUNSET EMBRACE** will go on sale during the first two weeks of January. Watch for an excerpt from this historical of spellbinding intensity in the backs of next month's LOVESWEPTS.

Since the other three novels by LOVESWEPT author's won't be published for such a long time, I'll mention them just briefly now and provide more details in months to come. In early April 1985 Iris Johansen's **THE FOR-EVER DREAM** goes on sale. A fervent love story against a background of a revolutionary scientific breakthrough and political scheming, this high voltage novel is set slightly in the future.

The eagerly anticipated next long work by Sharon and

(continued)

Tom Curtis will appear from Bantam on racks in July 1985. **SUNSHINE AND SHADOW** is so original in its premise and captivating in its execution that we are withholding description of this contemporary romantic novel for several months.

And, then, in November 1985 a remarkable gift goes out to you from Kay Hooper. **THE SUMMER OF THE UNICORN** is a breathtaking piece of romantic magic. Again, we won't reveal more about this novel until closer to publication date.

But, now, let's turn to the reading pleasure you can expect much sooner—namely, the four LOVESWEPTS for you next month.

Witty Billie Green brings us another sparkling romance in **THE COUNT FROM WISCONSIN,** LOVESWEPT #75. From the moment nearsighted cartoonist Kate Sullivan gets dashing Alex Delanore into focus, there is never a dull moment in their courtship. Whether at a magnificent villa in Monte Carlo or speeding through the French countryside after a shady character, Kate and Alex keep one another—and us!—enthralled. But beneath their wild attraction and tender revelations, there is a serious threat to their future together for, it seems, Kate and Alex are caught between two worlds.

Debuting in a new role as published author is our own Elizabeth Barrett with **TAILOR-MADE,** LOVESWEPT #76! A gently evocative love story of a young woman who has shunned the bright lights of Broadway for the tranquil beauty of New Hampshire, **TAILOR-MADE** has a divine hero in actor Daniel Collins. Playing Petruchio in the local summer stock production of *Kiss Me, Kate,* Daniel falls for Chris who is the costumer for the show . . . and finds his path to true love as rough as the one trod by the character he plays.

Nancy Holder strikes again with a thoroughly delightful, highly sensuous, totally off-the-wall love story in **FINDERS KEEPERS,** LOVESWEPT #77. Tender-hearted Allison Jones is a pet detective with a passionate commitment to mystery novels and movies of the 1940's. Heartbreaker David King is San Francisco's Most Eligible Bachelor, the owner of a fleet of limos, and a devoted gadgeteer. It's love at first sight for this unlikely duo . . . followed by a zany, emotion-wrenching clash of life styles that is gripping. I trust that like me you will leave your heart in San Francisco all right—in the roiling fog . . . under the Golden Gate bridge . . . with Allison and David.

What a reception you gave Barbara Boswell's first romance, **LITTLE CONSEQUENCES!** And, following up that successful inaugural bow. Barbara has created a marvelously offbeat romance in **SENSUOUS PERCEPTION,** LOVESWEPT #78. This book could be subtitled The Physicist Encounters the Psychic—but that doesn't really tip you to the fun and the touching emotion you'll experience in reading **SENSUOUS PERCEPTION.** Ashlee Martin has known for years that she's gifted with "second sight" and that as an adoptee she was separated at birth from her twin. Now she's searched out her lost sister Amber and is about to be reunited . . . though even her psychic abilities hadn't forewarned her about the devastating Locke, Amber's foster brother. Yankee Locke may have thought he was an expert in thermodynamic physics—but that was before he encountered Southern belle Ashlee whose mere presence inspires in him a dozen new theories about temperatures rising!

All of us at LOVESWEPT—authors and staff—send you our warmest wishes for a holiday season full of joy! Sincerely,

Carolyn Nichols

Carolyn Nichols
 Editor
LOVESWEPT
Bantam Books, Inc.
666 Fifth Avenue
New York, NY 10103

#1 HEAVEN'S PRICE
By Sandra Brown
Blair Simpson had enclosed herself in the fortress of her dancing, but Sean Garrett was determined to love her anyway. In his arms she came to understand the emotions behind her dancing. But could she afford the high price of love?

#2 SURRENDER
By Helen Mittermeyer
Derry had been pirated from the church by her ex-husband, from under the nose of the man she was to marry. She remembered every detail that had driven them apart—and the passion that had drawn her to him. The unresolved problems between them grew . . . but their desire swept them toward surrender.

#3 THE JOINING STONE
By Noelle Berry McCue
Anger and desire warred within her, but Tara Burns was determined not to let Damon Mallory know her feelings. When he'd walked out of their marriage, she'd been hurt.

Damon had violated a sacred trust, yet her passion for him was as breathtaking as the Grand Canyon.

#4 SILVER MIRACLES
By Fayrene Preston
Silver-haired Chase Colfax stood in the Texas moonlight, then took Trinity Ann Warrenton into his arms. Overcome by her own needs, yet determined to have him on her own terms, she struggled to keep from losing herself in his passion.

#5 MATCHING WITS
By Carla Neggers
From the moment they met, Ryan Davis tried to outmaneuver Abigail Lawrence. She'd met her match in the Back Bay businessman. And Ryan knew the Boston lawyer was more woman than any he'd ever encountered. Only if they vanquished their need to best the other could their love triumph.

#6 A LOVE FOR ALL TIME
By Dorothy Garlock
A car crash had left its marks on Casey Farrow's beauty. So what were Dan

Murdock's motives for pursuing her? Guilt? Pity? Casey had to choose. She could live with doubt and fear . . . or learn a lesson in love.

#7 A TRYST WITH MR. LINCOLN?

By Billie Green

When Jiggs O'Malley awakened in a strange hotel room, all she saw were the laughing eyes of stranger Matt Brady . . . all she heard were his teasing taunts about their "night together" . . . and all she remembered was nothing! They evaded the passions that intoxicated them until . . . there was nowhere to flee but into each other's arms.

#8 TEMPTATION'S STING

By Helen Conrad

Taylor Winfield likened Rachel Davidson to a Conus shell, contradictory and impenetrable. Rachel battled for independence, torn by her need for Taylor's embraces and her impassioned desire to be her own woman. Could they both succumb to the temptation of the tropi-

cal paradise and still be true to their hearts?

#9 DECEMBER 32nd . . . AND ALWAYS

By Marie Michael

Blaise Hamilton made her feel like the most desirable woman on earth. Pat opened herself to emotions she'd thought buried with her late husband. Together they were unbeatable as they worked to build the jet of her late husband's dreams. Time seemed to be running out and yet—would ALWAYS be long enough?

#10 HARD DRIVIN' MAN

By Nancy Carlson

Sabrina sensed Jacy in hot pursuit, as she maneuvered her truck around the racetrack, and recalled his arms clasping her to him. Was he only using her feelings so he could take over her trucking company? Their passion knew no limits as they raced full speed toward love.

#11 BELOVED INTRUDER

By Noelle Berry McCue

Shannon Douglas hated

Michael Brady from the moment he brought the breezes of life into her shadowy existence. Yet a specter of the past remained to torment her and threaten their future. Could he subdue the demons that haunted her, and carry her to true happiness?

and stayed to short-circuit her emotions? How could she choose between poetry and passion—between soul and Hart?

lar. But Maggie Sims and Mark Wilding were anything but perfectly matched. Maggie wanted to prove he was wrong about her. She knew they didn't belong together, but when he caressed her, she was swept up in a passion that promised a lifetime of love.

#17 TEMPEST AT SEA
By Iris Johansen
Jane Smith sneaked aboard playboy-director Jake Dominic's yacht on a dare. The muscled arms that captured her were inescapable—and suddenly Jane found herself agreeing to a month-long cruise of the Caribbean. Jane had never given much thought to love, but under Jake's tutelage she discovered its magic . . . and its torment.

#18 AUTUMN FLAMES
By Sara Orwig
Lily Dunbar had ventured too far into the wilderness of Reece Wakefield's vast Chilean ranch; now an oncoming storm thrust her into his arms . . . and he refused to let her go. Could he lure her, step by seductive step, away from the life she had forged for herself, to find her real home in his arms?

#19 PFARR LAKE AFFAIR
By Joan J. Domning
Leslie Pfarr hadn't been back at her father's resort for an hour before she was pitched into the lake by Eric Nordstrom! The brash teenager who'd made her childhood a constant torment had grown into a handsome man. But when he began persuading her to fall in love, Leslie wondered if she was courting disaster.

#20 HEART ON A STRING
By Carla Neggers
One look at heart surgeon Paul Houghton Welling told JoAnna Radcliff he belonged in the stuffy society world she'd escaped for a cottage in Pigeon Cove. She firmly believed she'd never fit into his life, but he set out to show her she was wrong. She was the puppet master, but he knew how to keep her heart on a string.

#21 THE SEDUCTION OF JASON
By Fayrene Preston
On vacation in Martinique, Morgan Saunders found Jason Falco. When a misunderstanding drove him away, she had to win him back. Morgan acted as a seductress, to tempt him to return; she sent him tropical flowers to tantalize him; she wrote her love in letters twenty feet high—on a billboard that echoed the words in her heart.

#22 BREAKFAST IN BED
By Sandra Brown
For all Sloan Fairchild knew, Hollywood had moved to San Francisco when mystery writer Carter Madison stepped into her bed-and-breakfast inn. In his arms the forbidden longing that throbbed between them erupted. Sloan had to choose—between her love for him and her loyalty to a friend . . .

#23 TAKING SAVANNAH
By Becky Combs
The Mercedes was headed straight for her! Cassie hurled a rock that smashed the antique car's taillight. The price driver Jake Kilrain exacted was a passionate kiss, and he set out to woo the Southern lady, Cassie, but discovered that his efforts to conquer the lady might end in his own surrender . . .

#24 THE RELUCTANT LARK
By Iris Johansen
Her haunting voice had earned Sheena Reardon fame as Ireland's mournful dove. Yet to Rand Challon the young singer was not just a lark but a woman whom he desired with all his heart. Rand knew he could teach her to spread her wings and fly free, but would her flight take her from him or into his arms forever?

#25 LIGHTNING THAT LINGERS
By Sharon and Tom Curtis
He was the Cougar Club's star attraction, mesmerizing hundreds of women with hips that swayed in the provocative motions

of love. Jennifer Hamilton offered her heart to the kindred spirit, the tender poet in him. But Philip's wordly side was alien to her, threatening to unravel the magical threads binding them . . .

#26 ONCE IN A BLUE MOON
By Billie Green
Arlie was reckless, wild, a little naughty—but in the nicest way! Whenever she got into a scrape, Dan was always there to rescue her. But this time Arlie wanted a very *personal* bailout that only *he* could provide. Dan never could say no to her. After all, the special favor she wanted was his own secret wish—wasn't it?

#27 THE BRONZED HAWK
By Iris Johansen
Kelly would get her story even if it meant using a bit of blackmail. She'd try anything to get inventor-genius Nick O'Brien to take her along in his experimental balloon. Nick had always trusted his fate to the four winds and the seven seas . . . until a feisty lady clipped his wings by losing herself in his arms . . .

#28 LOVE, CATCH A WILD BIRD
By Anne Reisser
Daredevil and dreamer, Bree Graeme collided with Cane Taylor on her family's farm—and there was an instant intimacy between them. Bree's wild years came to a halt, for when she looked into Cane's eyes, she knew she'd found love at last. But what price freedom to dare when the man she loved could rest only as she lay safe in his arms?

#29 THE LADY AND THE UNICORN
By Iris Johansen
Janna Cannon scaled the walls of Rafe Santine's estate, determined to appeal to the man who could save her animal preserve. She bewitched his guard dogs, then cast a spell over him as well. She offered him a gift he'd never dared risk reaching for before—but could he trust

his emotions enough to open himself to her love?

#30 WINNER TAKE ALL
By Nancy Holder
Holly Johnson was a powerful presence at the office, an unstoppable force on the racquetball court, and too much woman for the men she knew . . . until Dick DeWitt came into her life. A battle of wills and wits ensued, and to the victors the spoils were happiness and love.

#31 THE GOLDEN VALKYRIE
By Iris Johansen
Private detective Honey Winston had been duped into invading Prince Rubinoff's hotel suite. But behind the facade of the gossip columns' "Lusty Lance" she found an artist filled with longing. Would the gift of her love allow Lance to escape his gilded prison?

#32 C.J.'S FATE
By Kay Hooper
C.J. Adams had been teased about her lack of interest in men. On a ski trip with her friends she embraced a stranger, pretending they were secret lovers. Astonished at his reaction, she tried to nip their romance in the bud. But she'd met her match in a man who could answer her witty remarks and arouse in her a passionate need.

#33 THE PLANTING SEASON
By Dorothy Garlock
Iris had poured her energies into the family farm and the appearance of John Lang was unexpected. Suddenly the land was theirs to share. John wanted to prove his dedication and his feelings for Iris. But when disaster struck, it forced a confrontation that risked everything and taught Iris that only learning to grow together would bring them a harvest of love.

#34 FOR THE LOVE A SAMI
By Fayrene Preston
When heiress Sami Adkinson was arrested for demonstrating to save the seals, she begged attorney Daniel Parker-St. James

to bail her out. Daniel was smitten, soon cherishing Sami and protecting her from her fears. But holding onto Sami he found, was like trying to hug quicksilver . . .

#35 THE TRUSTWORTHY REDHEAD
By Iris Johansen
When Sabrina Courtney was hired to deliver birthday wishes to Alex ben Rashid, she wasn't warned that he had a weakness for redheads. From the moment he saw her, he wanted to possess her. Could a man who was used to getting what he wanted learn to trust the woman he loved?

#36 A TOUCH OF MAGIC
By Carla Neggers
A tragedy had made Sarah Blackstone president of her family's corporation. Promising herself one last fling, she bicycled to visit the Blackstones' old farm, only to find Brad "Magic" Craig, quarterback of the New York Novas. Brad tried to brand her as just another fan bent on seducing the Superbowl hero, but was the emotion between them real?

#37 IRRESISTIBLE FORCES
By Marie Michael
Shane McCallister considered the assignment of interviewing Nick Rutledge, the hero of the silver screen, a demotion. She resented having to profile a vain and shallow star. But she had her expectations shattered. Nick was intelligent, sensitive, and concerned about people and the land. And so the story she wrote had an irresistibly happy ending.

#38 TEMPORARY ANGEL
By Billie Green
When an explosion trapped Angie Jones and Senator Sam Clements in a cave for hours alone, her resistance to his charm weakened. But surely a Senator couldn't succeed if he were linked with a controversial writer like her! Angie hadn't counted on a filibuster—as Sam held fast to the angel who showed him the stars from close up . . .

#39 KIRSTEN'S INHERITANCE
By Joan J. Domning
Who was Dr. Cory Antonelli, and why did he have to come and claim his half of Aunt Ida's house? From the moment she found him asleep in her bed, Kirsten knew her cozy existence would never be the same. She bristled to find her life disturbed, but soon she knew an exhilarating love.
Would she and Cory fulfill Aunt Ida's long-ago dream?

#40 RETURN TO SANTA FLORES
By Iris Johansen
Jenny Cashman had long dreamed of declaring her love for Steve Jason, the casino owner who had adopted her as a young girl. She tried everything she could to make him see her for the woman she had become. Though he felt years older and much too jaded for her innocent love, Steve discovered that Jenny would never give herself to another man.

#41 THE SOPHISTICATED MOUNTAIN GAL
By Joan Bramsch
In costume Crissy Brant was transformed into Tulip Bloom, the saucy mountain gal. Toy manufacturer James Prince III fell for the backwoods charmer, but he grew to love the true Crissy, a sophisticate as well. They both were ornery cusses whose suspicion and stubbornness set them to feudin'—a fight only love could win.

#42 HEAT WAVE
By Sara Orwig
Marilee O'Neil piloted a hot air balloon into Cole Chandler's pool. But Cole rose to the occasion and took her in his arms, setting her afire with his impassioned embrace. In the hottest summer Kansas had seen in years, they set new heat records.

#43 TO SEE THE DAISIES . . . FIRST
By Billie Green
One moment Ben Garrison felt that his life was headed nowhere; then a woman wearing only a

trenchcoat changed everything! But the lovers weren't lost to an uncaring world . . . for her life was threatened by a man from the past she couldn't recall . . .

#44 NO RED ROSES
By Iris Johansen
When singer Rex Brody took Tamara Ledford in his arms, he knew the lady he'd been singing to all along was no longer a fantasy. But could he convince her that his feelings were sincere? Tamara rebelled, aching to return to her greenhouse and her precious herbs and flowers. Then Rex showered her with blossoms . . . but there were no red roses . . .

#45 THAT OLD FEELING
By Farene Preston
When she heard the waves crashing against the Baja coast, Lisa Saxon felt them echo within her heart. And when she turned to find Christopher, her ex-husband, her pulse quickened in frustration and desire. Could they dare to be honest, and make it for keeps this time?

#46 SOMETHING DIFFERENT
By Kay Hooper
Like her name, Gypsy had always preferred to roam the world at will, writing her books and loving the heroes who filled her dreams. But then architect Chase Mitchell slipped inside her heart to fulfill her fantasies. Gypsy and Chase resisted the happy ending the dream demanded— until a wily feline matchmaker found the keys to their love.

#47 THE GREATEST SHOW ON EARTH
By Nancy Holder
Melinda Franklin had a dream that wouldn't die: To keep hers an old-fashioned circus. Banker Evan Kessel arrived to review her loan application and ended up courting Melinda in the midst of her circus "family." How could a woman whose right palm revealed a heartline as big as the Grand Canyon resist him?

#48 BEWARE THE WIZARD
By Sara Orwig
A gorilla for a client? Straitlaced patent attorney Laurel Fortier couldn't believe it when toy inventor Thane Prescott appeared for their appointment covered with black fur and wearing a devilish grin under his shaggy mask. She was one lawyer who had no defenses against her very own "mad professor" of love.

#49 THE MAN NEXT DOOR
By Kathleen Downes
Jessica Winslow couldn't help overhearing the fight going on in the next cabin. Suddenly a door slammed, and a car raced away, stranding the man who'd lost the argument. She offered him dinner, and soon Ethan Jamieson was captivated by the gifted artist, whose paintings expressed her passionate soul.

#50 IN SEARCH OF JOY
By Noelle Berry McCue
Joy Barton had adored her foster brother Brent. She'd offered him her heart—and all of herself. But Brent had been afraid to take advantage of her sweetness. When he returned home after four years, Joy stood waiting, a woman now, with an undaunted passion that cried out for his love . . .

AN EXQUISITELY ROMANTIC NOVEL UNLIKE
ANY OTHER LOVE STORY YOU HAVE EVER READ

Chase the Moon

by
Catherine Nicholson

For Corrie Modena, only one man shares her dreams, a
stranger whom she has never met face to face and whom she
knows only as "Harlequin." Over the years, his letters sus-
tain her—encouraging, revealing, increasingly intimate. And
when Corrie journeys to Paris to pursue her music, she
knows that she will also be searching for her beloved
Harlequin. . . .

Buy CHASE THE MOON, on sale November 15, 1984,
wherever Bantam paperbacks are sold, or use the handy
coupon below for ordering:

A Dazzling New Novel

Scents

by
Johanna Kingsley

They were the fabulous Jolays, half sisters, bound by blood but not by love. Daughters of an outstanding French perfumer whose world had collapsed, now they are bitter rivals, torn apart by their personal quests for power. It was the luminous Vie who created an empire, but it was the sensuous, rebellious Marty who was determined to control it. No matter what the cost, she would conquer Vie's glittering world and claim it as her own . . .

Buy SCENTS, on sale December 15, 1984, wherever Bantam paperbacks are sold, or use the handy coupon below for ordering:

A TOWERING, ROMANTIC SAGA BY
THE AUTHOR OF
LOVE'S WILDEST FIRES

HEARTS
of
FIRE

by Christina Savage

For Cassie Tryon, Independence Day, 1776, signals a different kind of upheaval—the wild, unstoppable rebellion of her heart. For on this day, she will meet a stranger—a legendary privateer disguised in clerk's clothes, a mysterious man come to do secret, patriot's business with her father . . . a man so compelling that she knows her life will never be the same for that meeting. He is Lucas Jericho—outlaw, rebel, avenger of his family's fate at British hands, a man who is dangerous to love . . . and impossible to forget.

Buy HEARTS OF FIRE, on sale November 1, 1984, wherever Bantam paperbacks are sold, or use the handy coupon below for ordering:

A Stirring Novel of Destinies
Bound by Unquenchable Passion

SUNSET EMBRACE

by Sandra Brown

Fate threw Lydia Russell and Ross Coleman, two untamed outcasts, together on a Texas-bound wagon train. On that wild road, they fought the breathtaking desire blazing between them, while the shadows of their enemies grew longer. As the train rolled west, danger drew ever closer, until a showdown with their pursuers was inevitable. Before it was over, Lydia and Ross would face death . . . the truth about each other . . . and the astonishing strength of·their love.

Buy SUNSET EMBRACE, on sale January 15, 1985 wherever Bantam paperbacks are sold, or use the handy coupon below for ordering:

LOVESWEPT

Love Stories you'll never forget by authors you'll always remember

☐ 21603	**Heaven's Price #1** Sandra Brown	$1.95
☐ 21604	**Surrender #2** Helen Mittermeyer	$1.95
☐ 21600	**The Joining Stone #3** Noelle Berry McCue	$1.95
☐ 21601	**Silver Miracles #4** Fayrene Preston	$1.95
☐ 21605	**Matching Wits #5** Carla Neggers	$1.95
☐ 21606	**A Love for All Time #6** Dorothy Garlock	$1.95
☐ 21609	**Hard Drivin' Man #10** Nancy Carlson	$1.95
☐ 21610	**Beloved Intruder #11** Noelle Berry McCue	$1.95
☐ 21611	**Hunter's Payne #12** Joan J. Domning	$1.95
☐ 21618	**Tiger Lady #13** Joan Domning	$1.95
☐ 21613	**Stormy Vows #14** Iris Johansen	$1.95
☐ 21614	**Brief Delight #15** Helen Mittermeyer	$1.95
☐ 21616	**A Very Reluctant Knight #16** Billie Green	$1.95
☐ 21617	**Tempest at Sea #17** Iris Johansen	$1.95
☐ 21619	**Autumn Flames #18** Sara Orwig	$1.95
☐ 21620	**Pfarr Lake Affair #19** Joan Domning	$1.95
☐ 21621	**Heart on a String #20** Carla Neggers	$1.95
☐ 21622	**The Seduction of Jason #21** Fayrene Preston	$1.95
☐ 21623	**Breakfast In Bed #22** Sandra Brown	$1.95
☐ 21624	**Taking Savannah #23** Becky Combs	$1.95
☐ 21625	**The Reluctant Lark #24** Iris Johansen	$1.95

Prices and availability subject to change without notice.

Buy them at your local bookstore or use this handy coupon for ordering:

Bantam Books, Inc., Dept. SW, 414 East Golf Road, Des Plaines, Ill. 60016

Please send me the books I have checked above. I am enclosing
$_____ (please add $1.25 to cover postage and handling). Send
check or money order—no cash or C.O.D.'s please.

Mr/Ms_____

Address _____

City/State_____ Zip_____

SW—12/84

Please allow four to six weeks for delivery. This offer expires 6/85.

LOVESWEPT

Love Stories you'll never forget by authors you'll always remember

☐	21630	**Lightning That Lingers #25** Sharon & Tom Curtis	$1.95
☐	21631	**Once In a Blue Moon #26** Billie J. Green	$1.95
☐	21632	**The Bronzed Hawk #27** Iris Johansen	$1.95
☐	21637	**Love, Catch a Wild Bird #28** Anne Reisser	$1.95
☐	21626	**The Lady and the Unicorn #29** Iris Johansen	$1.95
☐	21628	**Winner Take All #30** Nancy Holder	$1.95
☐	21635	**The Golden Valkyrie #31** Iris Johansen	$1.95
☐	21638	**C.J.'s Fate #32** Kay Hooper	$1.95
☐	21639	**The Planting Season #33** Dorothy Garlock	$1.95
☐	21629	**For Love of Sami #34** Fayrene Preston	$1.95
☐	21627	**The Trustworthy Redhead #35** Iris Johansen	$1.95
☐	21636	**A Touch of Magic #36** Carla Neggers	$1.95
☐	21641	**Irresistible Forces #37** Marie Michael	$1.95
☐	21642	**Temporary Angel #38** Billie Green	$1.95
☐	21646	**Kirsten's Inheritance #39** Joan Domning	$2.25
☐	21645	**Return to Santa Flores #40** Iris Johansen	$2.25
☐	21656	**The Sophisticated Mountain Gal #41** Joan Bramsch	$2.25
☐	21655	**Heat Wave #42** Sara Orwig	$2.25
☐	21649	**To See the Daisies . . . First #43** Billie Green	$2.25
☐	21648	**No Red Roses #44** Iris Johansen	$2.25
☐	21644	**That Old Feeling #45** Fayrene Preston	$2.25
☐	21650	**Something Different #46** Kay Hooper	$2.25

Prices and availability subject to change without notice.